Purpose Me

Karina's Choice

Volume 3

Purpose Me

Karina's Choice

Volume 3

Seth Andre Robinson

HIGH BRIDGE
BOOKS & MEDIA

Contents

Bonus Chapters: Read the first three chapters of (*Purpose Me Volume 4*).

This book is dedicated to my ancestors and to the many upon many African people who weathered the storm of the slave trade and slavery. Their choice to hope and preserve is the reason why I am here today.

Prologue

"Ah, ah, ah," screams a six-year-old Karina. With both of her small hands balled tightly into fists, she pounds heavily upon a five-year-old boy named Victor. As he lies on the ground, he cries hysterically as he tries his best to shield his face from the vicious beating.

Karina and four other African boys were left behind when their homes and families became casualties of the slave trade. The slave trade was a horrible custom that was taking place in Ghana, Africa, during that time. After being rescued by a young Caucasian couple named Kevin and Ruth, Karina and the four boys were taken into their home and fostered by them. However, Karina and the boys didn't always get along.

While Karina continues to hit, she screams as well. Suddenly, she finds herself being pulled away from him.

"Okay, okay, take it easy!" she hears Kevin say. "Take it easy!"

Now completely in Kevin's possession, Karina screams even louder as she violently begins swinging her arms and feet.

Moments later, Karina sits quietly at a table that's located inside the cabin home of Kevin and Ruth. She had been made to sit there in order to calm her down. With dried tears still on her face, Karina looks across the room and sees Kevin standing near the bookcase. As he stands there, he reads a book with a wooden cover. Getting out of the chair, she goes over toward him and tries her best to get his attention by pulling on his pant leg.

Kevin, looking down, sees Karina looking up at him with a sorrowful look in her eyes.

Laughing, he asks, "Have you calmed down now?"

Karina nods her head, "Yes." She then points outside.

"Do you wish to go back outside?"

With a smile, Karina nods her head, "Yes," once more.

"Okay, we can go back outside."

Putting the book back on the shelf, Kevin takes Karina by the hand and begins heading toward the door. He and Karina are nearly out the door when Ruth suddenly calls.

"My love?"

"Yes, sweetheart."

"Might I have a word with you?"

Letting go of Karina's hand, Kevin draws close to Ruth to hear what she has to say.

"Yes, darling."

"We need to talk to the little girl to make sure that she understands what she did was wrong."

"Oh, Ruth, I know you are a teacher, so teaching is in your blood... but we cannot teach these children. They can't understand English, and the little girl cannot even speak at all.

"Well, we have to try Kevin. Little girl," Ruth then says to Karina. "Come," she tells her as she extends a hand. "Come."

With a confused look on her face, Karina walks slowly toward Ruth. Once there, Ruth takes her by the hand and sits her back at the table. She then says while motioning, "Hitting people is not nice, not nice." Karina, not comprehending Ruth's words, stares with a look of confusion. Ruth then begins to look around the room for a helpful way to communicate, and what comes into her view are two clear jars that are stationed above the stove. One is filled with salt and the other with brown sugar.

Going over to the shelf, Ruth picks up the jars and then sits back at the table. She then places the jars in front of her and side by side. "Salt and sugar," Ruth then says to Karina as she points to each jar. "Salt... and sugar," she says once more. Ruth then removes the lids of the jars, and after removing them, she puts a dab of salt on her finger and says to Karina while tasting, "Salt, uh, bitter." She then puts a dab of sugar on her finger and says while tasting, "But sugar, ummm, sweet!" She then moves the jars closer to Karina and says while pointing, "You... pick one. You can be bitter, or you can be sweet; you can be mean, or you can be nice."

Kevin, looking on, kindly says, "That was a very nice lesson, Ruth."

"Thank you, Kevin," she looks at him and replies with a gentle smile

"But she will not understand all of that," he sarcastically adds.

"Oh, Kevin, why must you be so pessimistic?"

"I'm not being pessimistic, Ruth, I'm just being realistic."

"Well, I'm just being hopeful."

"I know Ruth," he says in a derogatory tone, "I know... you're just being hopeful... you always... got to be... hopeful. But what you got is your head stuck in the clouds."

As Ruth gets up from the table to respond, she and Kevin begin to argue.

As Ruth and Kevin continue to converse, Karina picks up the jar of salt, looks at it, then puts it back down on the table. She then picks up the jar of sugar and with the jar of sugar still in her hand, she looks at Kevin and Ruth and says... "*Sweet.*"

Chapter 1

TEN YEARS LATER, KARINA, AS WELL AS THE FOUR BOYS, have now been adopted by Kevin and Ruth. It's a summer evening of August 14, 1808, and a now sixteen-year-old Karina stands in a garden that's located in back of her new home. As she stands there, she intensely watches a butterfly that has landed on the tip of her fingers.

"Karina!" she suddenly hears Ruth calling from inside the house.

"Yef," she answers.

"Please come inside and help me prepare for supper."

"Yef."

As she lifts her hand in the air, the butterfly takes off and flies away. She then turns and heads inside the house. Once there, Karina sees an older-looking Ruth at the stove.

"Here," says Ruth as she hands her a stack of dishes, "Set the table."

"Yef."

"Oh, and Karina?"

"The word is *yes*, Karina, not yef. Do my ears have the pleasure of hearing you say the word correctly?"

"Y-ess," she slowly pronounces, "Mother," she then says, "I apologize for not saying the word correctly."

"No need to apologize, Karina, for you have come a long way from not being able to speak at all, but now *you are* speaking, and your speech is getting better every day."

"Thankf to you," Karina tells her. "You taught me how to peak—I mean, *speak*."

With a slight laugh, Ruth gives Karina a pat on the shoulder and then a kiss on the cheek.

Just then, three of the four boys that Kevin and Ruth adopted (named Emmanuel, Joshua, and Daniel) enter the house. They appear to be out of breath and sweaty, yet smiles adorn their faces.

"Did you boys enjoy playing kickball with your father and brothers?" Ruth asks.

"Well, *we* enjoyed it," says a nineteen-year-old Emmanuel happily.

"But we're not sure if father and our younger brothers did," adds an eighteen-year-old Daniel as he laughs a little.

"Here they come now," a seventeen-year-old Joshua adds.

An older and bearded Kevin enters the house, and gloomily trailing behind him is a fifteen-year-old Victor. Walking beside Victor are Kevin and Ruth's nine-year-old birth son named Bryan.

Noticing the glum look on their faces, Karina asks, "Guyz, whatz wrong?"

"Me, Joshua, and Daniel played against them three, and they lost," Emmanuel tells her.

"That's because you guys cheated," Victor yells.

"Victor, for the umpteenth time... *we did not cheat*!!!"

"Okay, Emmanuel," Ruth then says, "Okay, there's no need to shout. Honestly, you must control that temper of yours."

"Temper... what temper?" Emmanuel then calmly responds, "I don't have a temper. I'm just speaking very loudly since my dear younger brother is hard of hearing."

"Hum, he also must control his sarcasm," Kevin interjects

"But Emmanuel is right," Joshua says, "We didn't cheat; we won fair and square... we're just better at kickball than you."

"Okay, Joshua," says Kevin, "let's not be cocky. Especially in light of the fact that it was I who taught you and your brothers how to play kickball in the first place."

"Yes, Joshua," says Ruth, "stay humble! Remember what the good book says about pride: that pride always comes before a fall. But enough of the kickball talk. Let's sit down and have supper."

"Victor, sit next to me!" Bryan eagerly says to him as he grabs his hand.

"Okay, little brother," Victor responds with a laugh. However, just before sitting, Victor pulls out a chair for his mother.

"Awww, thank you, Victor," she tells him as she takes her seat. "You are such a sweetheart."

"Cabbage!" Victor then shouts as he sees the dish sitting on the table. "I love cabbage!"

"Me too!" says Bryan

Victor, still excited by the sight of his favorite dish, begins to sit down but misses his chair and falls to the floor.

"Must you always be so clumsy?" Daniel laughs as he shakes his head.

"Leave Victor alone!" Bryan shouts

"Yes, leave your brother alone, Daniel," says Ruth. "And Bryan, I know you love your big brother dearly and don't want anyone picking on him, but no shouting at the table." Ruth then looks to Karina. "Karina," she says, "It's your turn to bless the meal."

"Yef, Mother. I mean, *y-ess*."

Once heads are bowed and eyes are closed, Karina begins to pray. "Dear Lod… blet this food… in your name… ah-men."

As the family opens their eyes and begins fixing their plates, Daniel laughs as he mockingly repeats, "Blet this food." Upon hearing his mimicry, the rest of the boys begin to laugh.

"Okay, boys," says Ruth, "That will be enough."

However, the laughing persists.

"Boys!" Kevin then shouts in an authoritative voice, "Stop!" Upon hearing their father's command, the laughter comes to an end. "And you, Daniel," Kevin then says. "You are always teasing your sister. Stop it!"

"Yes, Father."

Kevin picks up a fork to eat, but suddenly he looks beside him and sees Karina sitting at the table with her head down.

Seeing the sight causes Kevin's mind to flash back to a conversation he and Ruth once had when they first adopted the children. Kevin remembers a time when he and Ruth were standing in the main area of the house, and as they stood there, they watched the children as they slept by the fireplace.

"They are all our children now," he recalls hearing Ruth say.

"Yes, they are," Kevin concurs

"And they have been through a lot, losing their families and their homes to that horrible slave trade."

"Yes, a lot has happened to them."

"But we cannot feel sorry for them Kevin; we cannot even allow them to feel sorry for themselves, for it would cripple them."

"I agree."

As the memory fades, Kevin's eyes fall back on Karina, who's still sitting at the table with her head down.

"Karina," Kevin then calls.

"Y-ess."

"No feeling sorry for yourself, you hear?"

"Yes, Father."

Karina begins eating, still with her head down and a pitiful look on her face. Suddenly, she feels Kevin's fingers on the tip of her chin, and with his fingers, he gently faces her head toward him. He then places his hand underneath her chin, and after doing so, he raises her head back up. Karina, now looking at her father full face, sees him give a wink... then a smile. Catching onto his gesture, Karina smiles in return. With her head now up, she resumes eating.

After dinner, the family sings while sitting in front of the fireplace. As they continue to sing, Kevin plays the guitar and Karina the piano. However, their singing is interrupted when...

Chapter 2

KARINA HITS AN OFF KEY ON THE PIANO. "KARINA," THE boys whine, "you messed up the song."

"Sorry."

The family resumes singing, when Karina hits an off key once more. "My goodness, Karina," Daniel then says as he laughs. "You sure do mess up a lot."

"Daniel," Ruth then says, "You are being rather rude."

"I agree," says Kevin. "Apologize to your sister."

'Sorry," he says with reluctance.

"Say it like you mean it, young man!" Ruth sternly tells him.

"I am sorry," he then says with compassion.

"And Karina." Ruth looks at her and says, "Do not allow for your brother's words to hurt you, you hear?"

"Y-ess, Mother. I hear you."

"You have come a long way with your piano playing."

"Thanks to you, Mother. You taught me how to play."

"Well, praise the Lord and thanks be to God who touched Bishop Amare's heart to give us this piano. Now let us prepare our hearts for a reading from God's word. But first, let us say our proclamation."

Everyone then says, "I am a child of God. I am fearfully and wonderfully made. I am attractive, intelligent, and strong. I do have the power to show self-control; this is my mindset."

"Very well," says Ruth. She then opens a Bible, but before she reads, she says, "Now, in our lifetime, we will all have problems, problems that seem just like troubled waters. And sometimes, God will move those troubled waters out of our way like he did for Moses and the children of Israel when they were at the Red Sea. Sometimes, God will cause us to rise above and walk on those troubled waters like he did for Peter when he and the other disciples were stuck out in the middle of the deep. But then there are times when God will just make sure we have a paddle and a boat."

"Mother, what do that mean?" Karina asks.

"Karina, sometimes God will not move problems out of our way or even cause us to rise above them. Sometimes he will simply give us the strength we need to endure. So, the next time you experience a problem… ask God to reveal his will for the situation and then ask him to give you the strength to accept it. Philippians 4:12–13," she then says as she begins to read, but Daniel interjects.

"I know what it says. I memorized it by heart so can I say it!"

"Okay, Daniel, go ahead… say it."

"Philippians 4:12–13: I know what it is to be in need, and I know what it is to have plenty. I have learned the secret of being content in any and every situation, whether well-fed or hungry, whether living in plenty or in want. I can do all this through him who gives me strength."

"Very good, Daniel," Ruth tells him.

"Impressive," Kevin tells him.

While Ruth and Kevin praise Daniel for his memorizing skills, Karina looks to the floor to ponder the lesson her mother just gave.

Chapter 3

LATER THAT NIGHT, AS KARINA LIES IN HER BED AND STARES at the ceiling, her mind dwells on the hurtful words she heard from Daniel during the day. As she feels the silver necklace that was once given to her by Ruth, she remembers hearing Daniel say in a mocking tone while sitting at the dinner table, "Blet this food." She then recalls him saying, "Karina, you sure do mess up a lot."

"You are right," she then says aloud, "Thou do meff up a lot."

Her train of thought is then interrupted by a knock at her bedroom door.

"Yef," she answers as she sits up and places her feet on the cold wooden floor.

"It's Mother," says the voice on the other side of the door, "May I enter?"

"Yef.,"

"And it is *yes*, Karina," says Ruth as she makes her way into the room. "Not yef. Do my ears have the pleasure of hearing you say the word correctly?"

"Ye-ss."

"Very well. There's a slight chill in the air tonight," says Ruth as she goes towards the window to close the drapes. "Came to see if you are warm, daughter." She then says as she notices the sad expression on Karina's face, "What troubles you tonight?"

"Not troubled, Mother. I am well."

"Oh, don't sell me a wet dog, Karina. You are indeed troubled tonight. What troubles you tonight?" She asks as she sits beside her. "Tell me."

"I wonder about s-ome thingf tonight."

"What do you wonder about?" she asks as she lightly strokes Karina's long black wool hair.

"How if it is that I cannot f-f-f-peak properly?" Karina says as tears begin to run down her dark-complexioned face. "I alone in this family have such a har-har-hard-ship. Why-why-why me?"

"You stutter whenever thou art overwhelmed. Ease yourself, daughter," she tells her as she wipes the tears from her face. "Ease yourself, so that you may be able to speak."

Inhaling, then exhaling, Karina makes another attempt to convey her feelings.

"How is-s it that I cannot s-peak properly? I alone have thi-s hardship, and I know, Mother, that you and Father have said not to feel sorry for myself, but the pain of me not f-peaking properly and being mocked even by my own brothers truly hurt-s me. Sometimes, I wonder: Does God love me? Does he care about me? If so, then why must he allow for me to have such a hardship? Was it not enough for me to have my birth family taken away from me, must I now suffer mockery due to my speech?"

"God Almighty, my child," says Ruth as tears appear in her own eyes. "You are filled with such sadness, and it grieves me to see you in such pain. But listen to my words so that your soul may be comforted. I know the mockery given to you by your brothers tonight was painful indeed, and I know when you lost your birth family, that was even more painful. The reason why God has allowed you to experience such pain is yet to be known. But God does love you, or else he would not have allowed for your father and me to find you. Don't be discouraged, for God surely has a purpose for you."

"Purpose... me?"

"Yes, Karina. God truly has a purpose for your life."

"What plan does God possibly has for me?"

"Well... I believe that God will use you to speak."

"Me f-peak?" she responds with a slight laugh.

"Yes, Karina. God will use you to speak."

"Oh Mother, I know you are trying to comfort me, and I thank you for that. But I find it hard to believe in what you are telling me."

"I know you might find it hard to receive right now, but just yield yourself to his plan. You will be pleasantly surprised by what God can do through you if you just submit yourself to him. Now let me help you under the covers," she tells her as she begins helping Karina under the blanket.

"I love you, Karina," she says as she gives her a kiss on the forehead.

"I love you too, Mother," Karina responds as she renders a slight smile.

"Now, try to get some rest."

As Ruth begins leaving the room, Karina lies in bed and stares at the ceiling. While doing so, the words her mother just spoke play back in her mind. "You will be pleasantly surprised by what God can do through you if you just submit yourself to him."

Seconds later, as Ruth enters the living room, she sees Kevin sitting by the fireplace while talking to Emmanuel.

"Just think about what I said," she hears Kevin say to Emmanuel as he stands to his feet

"Okay, Father," says Emmanuel. He then heads towards his bedroom.

After watching Emmanuel enter his room and close the door behind him, Kevin looks and sees Ruth standing near Karina's door

"Hello, my love. Is everything okay with Karina? It sounded like she was upset."

"She was, but I talked to her, so she's better now. What was going on with you and Emmanuel?"

"I was just talking to him about his temper and trying to figure out why he's so angry all the time. Thought if I understood, I could help him better. I tell you, Ruth, sometimes I worry about our children. Not sure if they're going to be okay."

"There you go again being Mr. Pessimistic."

"I'm not Ruth, I'm just being…"

"Realistic, I know. But you need not worry. God has his hands on our children."

"It's just that you have Emmanuel and his temper, Joshua with his bragging, and Daniel with his constant teasing," Kevin tells her.

"But then there's Victor," Ruth interjects. "He's a sweet kid."

"Yeah, he is a sweet kid," Kevin says as he looks to the side and smiles, "just clumsy sometimes."

"He can be, but Bryan just loves him *so* much," says Ruth. "He can't stand to be without his big brother, not for one second. He wants to go everywhere he goes, do everything he does, and he even repeats everything Victor says."

"Me too!" Kevin adds with a laugh as he mimics Bryan. "And Karina?" Kevin then asks, "What are your thoughts on her?"

"God has something special for Karina."

"Yeah?"

"Yeah."

"I just wish she wouldn't get so down on herself every time Daniel picks on her. You and I both know that this world is not very kind. And we can try our best to shield her from pain, but we can't do that all the time, Ruth. At some point, she's going to have to learn how to be strong and be strong on her own."

"You're right. She must learn how to be strong. We must pray that God will give her the strength she needs to persevere. So, can we do that tonight, Kevin? Can we spend some time praying? And not just for her but for all our children. Can we?"

"Yes, my love... We can."

Upon hearing Kevin's words, Ruth joins Kevin at the fireplace. Once there, they join hands and pray.

***

Hours later, Karina is shaken awake.

"Karina, Karina," calls a woman with a southern accent. "Rise up outta that bed, child, and come wit' me!"

Sitting up, Karina sees a woman of dark complexion standing at her bedroom doorway. Dressed in tattered clothing, she says to her, "I'm fixin' to show you somethin' spe-chal. So, get outta that bed, child, and come wit' me!" As the woman turns and leaves the room, a black branded mark on the upper left corner of her back grabs Karina's attention.

"I do not know that woman, and her speech is strange."

"Karina, come on," she then hears the woman shout from outside her bedroom.

Upon hearing the woman's shout, Karina quickly gets out of bed and runs into the other room. "God Almighty," she then stops and shouts. "What is this that is piercing my feet?" she questions as she lifts a foot from the ground to check the piercing.

Looking down, Karina sees that her feet are posed on a dusty ground that's covered with pine needles and cones. "Are my eyes deceiving me? Did I not f-weep, I mean sweep this floor before I went to bed? Let me s-weep this floor once more before mother sees it and punishes me."

She begins to get the broom, but in a split-second, stops. "Oh my," she then says with her eyes open wide. Looking, Karina sees that she's now standing in the midst of a nightly wooded forest adorned with tall pine trees. "Thif if not the room in which the family sits... where am I?"

"Karina," then sees the woman calling from a few feet ahead. "Come wit' me!"

The woman then turns and begins walking forward, but Karina remains in place. "How can it be that I be s-s- standing in the midst of a fo-reft and not the room where the family sits?" says Karina as she looks up at the tall trees. "And thif fo-reft loo-ks s-s-so s-cary at night." A sudden breeze that blows causes the trees to move like creatures in the night. "Wait!" she then exclaims as she runs toward the woman. "Wait for me!" Karina, now directly behind the woman, asks, "So where are we going?"

"Hold your horses, child. You'll see."

"Hold my horses?" Karina whispers in question, "What is she talking about? I don't have any horses."

Suddenly, the flickering of a yellow and orange light is seen up ahead. Judging from the bonfires she experienced with her family, Karina perceives that the flickering light is more like a burning flame. As she draws closer, the growing intensity of the heat accommodated by the sparks flying in the crisp night air gives way to her perception.

Silhouettes of people sitting around the fire come into view. However, the only sound that can be heard coming from inside the circle is the crackling sound the fire makes as it strikes the logs.

Now, among the people, Karina notices that there's a look of weariness on each and every person's face.

"God Almighty," she then says as tears well up in her eyes. "There if s-uch a feeling of hope-less-ness here. I can feel it."

"And that is why I brought you here, Karina," the woman says to her. "I brought you here so you can talk to these people

"Me... speak? I cannot... speeeak," she sounds as she suddenly feels a presence passing through her. Looking, Karina sees that what has passed through her is the spirit of a woman who is of dark complexion. Dressed in tattered clothing, her jet-black hair is stuffed under a pale gold turban. As the spirit of this woman stands in the midst of the people, she says with strength in her voice, "Let us always do what we can to keep hope alive."

"Mama?" Karina questions while looking at the spirit, "Is that you?"

"No, Karina," the woman tells her. "That's not your birth mother... look closer."

For a moment, Karina gives the spirit a hard glance. "Huh," she then gasps as she covers her mouth, "If that me?"

"Yes, Karina, it's you… or at least it can be."

"But how can that be? That woman who s-peaks to thif people s-s-speaks with much s- trength in her voice, and her speech is plain. I myself am fearful to speak in front of others, for in my speech I stammer, and my words are never spoken correctly."

"That might be so, Karina, but all things are possible if you just believe. So, do you, Karina?" The woman then asks, "Do you believe that that can be you?"

Upon hearing the question, Karina begins backing away slowly. "No," her voice barely ghosting between her lips. "No," she shakes her head. "No!" she then screams as she runs back towards her bedroom. Now inside, Karina jumps into bed and pulls the covers over her head.

"Karina," a female voice call.

"No… I'm not f-peaking to no crowd of people," she responds with the covers still over her head.

"Karina," the voice calls once more.

"I said n-n-no," she shouts as she removes the covers. "I'm not f-peaking to no crowd of…"

Looking, she sees her mother standing at her bedroom doorway with a confused look on her face.

"I understand," Ruth then says. "And you do not have to *speak* to no crowd of people, but you do have to get out of bed and get ready for breakfast."

As Karina turns and places her feet on the cold wooden floor, her mother says, "Oh and Karina."

"Ye-ss, Mother."

"It's speak, not fpeak. Do my ears have the pleasure of hearing you say the word correctly?"

"S-peak," she slowly pronounces.

"Very well. Now get ready for breakfast."

As Karina continues to sit on the edge of the bed, she looks to the floor, and while doing so, the words the woman spoke to her in the dream play back in her mind. "So do you, Karina? Do you believe that that can be you?" She continues to ponder the woman's words when suddenly, Karina hears…

Chapter 4

EMMANUEL, DANIEL, AND JOSHUA ARE SCREAMING. standing to her feet, Karina goes toward her bedroom doorway to inquire about the commotion. Looking, she sees Victor and Bryan running from her brothers' bedroom with wet but empty wooden pails in their hands. As they run and laugh, a drenched Emmanuel, Daniel, and Joshua chase after them.

Ruth looks on while shaking her head and shouts, "Stop running in the house!"

Upon hearing her words, Victor and Bryan run outside with their brothers running after them. Ruth then notices Karina says, "Can you believe this?"

"What happened?" Karina asks.

"Bryan and Victor decided to wake your brothers up this morning by dumping cold water on them. I guess it was payback for them beating them in kickball yesterday. Honestly... your brothers are something el..." but she stops talking when she looks and sees Kevin slowly emerging from the boys' room with an empty water bucket and a paranoid look on his face.

"You too?" Ruth asks in disbelief

"Just having some fun," Kevin lightly tells her.

Shaking her head and rolling her eyes, Ruth laughs while saying, "Well, do you think you and your sons can stop having fun for a moment so we can have breakfast?"

"Yes, we can. I'll go and get them."

"Thank you."

As Kevin leaves the house, Ruth looks at Karina and laughs once more. "Well, good morning," she then says.

"Good morning," Karina replies. She then walks over to the kitchen table and sits down.

"So, what was going on with you this morning? Why were you under the covers and shouting about not speaking to no crowd of people?"

"I guess I was just having a strange dream."

"Really, about what?"

"Well… in my dream, I saw myself in a strange place. I was speaking to a crowd of people, and when I spoke, my voice was strong and my speech was plain."

"God almighty, really? Do you think this dream was a dream of what's to come?"

"Oh Mother, I pray not. For in this dream, these people were in a desolate place, and I felt in the dream that I was right there with them."

At that moment, Kevin and the boys came inside the house.

"We'll finish talking later," Ruth whispers to Karina. She then goes toward the stove.

"Okay, family," says Ruth as she turns from the stove with a basket full of cornbread, "I made nice warm cornbread for breakfast this morning." After setting it down on the table, Ruth has a seat. She then asks Victor to lead in grace. After Victor finishes praying, Karina and the boys begin to partake. "So… how does it taste?"

"Good!" the boys simultaneously say.

"Karina." Ruth then looks at her and asks, "What do you think about the cornbread?"

With a finger in her mouth, Karina removes it and says, "Sweet."

Upon hearing Karina's response, Ruth and Kevin look at each other and begin to laugh.

"What?" Karina questions

"That was actually your very first word," Kevin tells her, "Re-member?"

Karina looks to the side in order to recall the moment. "I remember," she then replies as she renders a smile.

"So…" Ruth then asks as she sits at the table, "what is everybody going to do today?"

"We can play kickball again!" says Joshua.

"Why?" Kevin laughs, "so you can brag if you beat me? No, thank you. Besides, I have errands to run for the orphanage today."

"Speaking of the orphanage," says Ruth, "We are set as a family to help serve dinner there this evening."

The boys groan.

"I like working at the orphanage," Victor says joyfully.

"Me too," says Bryan.

"Surely you guys would," says Emmanuel sarcastically as he shakes his head.

"Well, maybe before we go to the orphanage we can go for a walk in the fo-reft," says Karina.

"Fo-reft," Daniel says in an undertone as he shakes his head and laughs.

"It's a beautiful day," Karina goes on to say. "We can go right after breakfast."

"Yes, let us do that!" says Victor.

"Yes, let us do that!" Bryan repeats.

"Well, they can, but you, Bryan Hopkins, cannot," Ruth sternly tells him.

"Aww, why not?"

"Because you have schoolwork to catch up on, young man. I let it go yesterday since it was Sunday, but not today. And Karina, the word is *forest*, not fo-reft. Do my ears have the pleasure of hearing you say the word correctly?"

"For-rest," she slowly pronounces.

"Very good."

"Mother, may I please go to the forest with Victor?" Bryan pleads. "Please!"

"Not today. You must finish your school work."

"Okay," Bryan gloomily responds.

"Aww, do not be down, little brother," Victor then tells him. "You and I will play kickball when I return."

"You promise?" says Bryan as he begins to perk up.

"Yes, I promise."

"And I promise too," Joshua suddenly says, "to get you guys back after throwing buckets of cold water on us this morning."

"Serves you right after bragging about winning kickball yesterday," Kevin tells him. "You always got to brag."

"Yeah," Victor says with a smirk. "And besides, you won't be able to catch me anyway. I'm too fast for you!"

"Well, you're not too fast for me now," says Joshua as he reaches across the table to grab him. As Victor quickly moves away, he accidentally knocks the cornbread out of Emmanuel's hand.

"Victor!" Emmanuel shouts as his cornbread hits the floor. "You clumsy fool. Look what you made me do!"

"Sorry," Victor responds as he looks at Emmanuel with glazed eyes.

"Okay, Emmanuel, calm down," says Ruth. "Just get another piece," she tells him as she hands him the basket filled with cornbread. "And no frolicking at the table, Joshua… you know better."

"Sorry," he responds.

The family quietly resumes eating breakfast when suddenly Daniel jokingly blurts out, "He called him a clumsy fool."

Upon hearing his remark, Karina and her brothers begin to laugh.

"That's not funny," Ruth says to them, but the laughter persists. "Kevin," Ruth then looks at him and says, "Tell the children to …" But she stops talking when she notices Kevin is laughing as well. "Victor." She then looks at him and says, "Victor, don't worry about your bro…" But she stops once more when she sees that Victor is now laughing as well. Inhaling then exhaling, Ruth shakes her head and says, "Well… clumsy fool," and with the words uttered, the laughter at the table grows even louder.

"Victor might be clumsy," then says Daniel to Emmanuel, "but why he gotta be a fool?"

"I don't know," Emmanuel replies. "Why does he have to be a fool… I ask myself that question every day."

Everyone resumes eating; however, the laughter at the table persists.

After breakfast, as Karina and her brothers make their way out of the house, Bryan walks beside Victor with his arms tightly wrapped around his waist.

"I want to go with you," Bryan whines.

"I know, little brother, but you have to stay here and finish your schoolwork. We'll play kickball when I return… okay?"

"Okay."

Karina and her brothers begin making their way toward the forest. Karina, looking back, waves goodbye as she shouts, "See you later."

"See you later," Kevin, Ruth, and Bryan simultaneously say.

Karina continues heading toward the forest when suddenly she gets an odd feeling in the pit of her stomach.

"Dear Lord," she then stops and whispers, "why am I suddenly getting an uneasy feeling about this journey?" She ponders the thought as she looks to the ground. "Perhaps, I'm just being fearful, Karina," she then says as she begins to laugh. She begins walking forward when suddenly she looks and sees a tall man dressed in a white robe looking at her.

Rendering a slight smile, he has jet black hair and smooth, dark skin. Stopping in place, Karina says as she continues to stare in awe, "You look fa-mil-iar... where have I seen you before?"

A flashback quickly enters her mind as she remembers seeing the man sitting on the rock in her village when she was a little girl.

"Karina come on!" she then hears Emmanuel shout.

"Coming!" she shouts in return as she glances forward. Looking back to where she saw the man standing, she now sees him nowhere in sight.

Looking perplexed, Karina resumes walking forward.

Moments later, after reaching the forest, Victor takes off running.

"Yeah, you better run," says Joshua as he sees Victor running away. "But don't worry," he then shouts, "sooner or later, I will catch you."

"What a lovely day to be in the fo-reft," says Karina as she looks up and around with a smile on her face.

"Foreft," Daniel repeats with laughter.

"Daniel, leave Karina alone," Emmanuel shouts. "You are always picking on her; leave her alone!"

"Well, why must she always say words incorrectly. Karina! The word is *forest,* not fo-reft. Do my ears have the pleasure of hearing you say the word correctly?" he adds with a sarcastic grin on his face as he mocks his mother, Ruth.

Upon hearing Daniel's words, Karina begins putting her head down.

"Don't do that, Sis," Emmanuel tells Karina when he sees her putting her head down, "Don't let Daniel's words break your spirit."

"Ahhh!" They suddenly hear Victor scream.

"That was Victor's scream," Karina says to her brothers as she raises her head back up. "Victor," Karina calls out, but she doesn't get an answer.

"Victor?" Emmanuel then shouts. But still, no response.

Karina and her brothers then take off running in the direction from which they heard Victor's scream. Once there, they see...

Chapter 5

VICTOR IS LYING UNCONSCIOUS ON THE GROUND.
"Victor!" screams Karina as she draws close to him, but he doesn't respond. "Victor!" she screams once more, but still he remains unresponsive. Kneeling by his side, she begins shaking him, when unexpectedly, Emmanuel screams and falls to the ground… then Daniel… then Joshua.

Standing to her feet, Karina looks confusedly at her brothers lying on the ground. "What is going on here?" Her eyes are then drawn to a few feet ahead of her, as she looks… and sees… the tall, dark-skinned man in the white robe staring at her. "You again?" says Karina as she stares at the man with a perplexed look on her face.

"Sorry," he says sadly.

"Sar-ry… for what?"

Suddenly, Karina feels a sharp pain on the side of her neck. Reaching her hand to where the pain is, Karina feels a small stick piercing the side of her neck. Pulling the stick out, she looks and realizes she's just been hit by a wooden tranquilizer. As she continues to stare at the dart, she finds herself beginning to feel lightheaded. Then, without warning, her legs give way, causing her to fall to the ground. Karina, now lying on the ground with her left cheek planted firmly into the dirt, sees a blurry vision of African men with painted faces coming toward her. As the men begin to pick her up, she loses consciousness.

Chapter 6

MOMENTS LATER, KARINA OPENS HER EYES. AS SHE sits up and looks around, she realizes that she's now trapped inside of a wooden cage that's made out of thick branches. She gasps when she looks and realizes she's been stripped of all clothing. Upon her discovery, she quickly moves to the corner of the cage, draws her knees close to her body, then wraps her arms tightly around them.

As she sits and trembles, she looks over to her left and sees outside the cage her four brothers. Still unconscious, they are stripped of all clothing and individually tied to a tree.

Karina then hears talking in the distance. Looking over to her right, she sees a heavy-set African man. Dressed in a royal purple Kenta cloth, he wears a small gold crown on the top of his head. She sees the African king engaging in a conversation with a European officer. As they continue to converse, the men turn and begin walking toward Karina's brothers. As they approach each individual, the officer inspects them. They then approach Karina's cage. Once there, the officer looks inside. "You capture some really good prisoners." The officer tells the king, "They're young, healthy, and strong: a trade worth making."

"So, you'll take them?" the king asks with a desperate look in his eyes.

"Yes, we'll take them," the officer replies. "Bring the prisoners to the coast of Guinea. There they will be held in a dungeon until we set sail."

The officer then turns and begins walking away. "And our deal?" the king then asks the officer.

Stopping, the officer turns and says to him, "We will conduct our trade once we receive the prisoners." He then turns and resumes walking away.

Once the soldier has left, the African king takes another look inside Karina's cage. "Get your rest, young girl. You have a long journey ahead of you." Slightly laughing, he then turns and walks away.

"Thif… thif hass to be a dream," Karina then says to herself with tears in her eyes. "A… a, bad, bad dream. Mother, call me so that I may wake up from this terrible dream. Please, Mother, call me!" However, her mother doesn't call. Inhaling, then exhaling, Karina goes into the corner of the cage.

Still sitting on the ground, she presses both her knees close to her body, then tightly wraps her arms around them.

Chapter 7

BACK AT THE CABIN, AS RUTH SITS BY THE FIREPLACE, SHE stares deep into the burning fire. "Mother," Bryan then calls as he approaches her from behind, "where are Victor and the rest of them? When are they coming home? It's almost dark."

With teary eyes, Ruth takes Bryan by the hand, sits him on her lap, and holds him close. Suddenly, the front door opens, and in comes a distraught-looking Kevin.

Noticing the look on his face, Ruth stands with Bryan. She then says to him, "Bryan, please go to your room so I might have a word with your father in private."

"Where's Victor, Karina, and the rest of them?" he asks as he looks at his mother and then at his father.

"Bryan, please listen to your mother," Kevin tells him.

"Okay," he gloomily responds. Putting his head down, he makes his way to his room.

Once Bryan has gone into his room, Kevin says with teary eyes, "I looked everywhere, Ruth… everywhere! I even asked some of the workers from the orphanage to help me, and they searched all through the forest and couldn't find a trace of them anywhere. And we had no choice but to retire since it was getting dark."

"Oh, don't worry, my love," says Ruth as she draws close to give Kevin a hug. "They probably lost their way and decided to huddle up somewhere together."

"Ruth, they've been to that forest over a hundred times already!"

"I know, but rest assured, they will return," she replies with a smile plastered on her face. "Remember what we always say to each other in troubled times… He is God of the sunshine; he is God of the rain. He is God in the light, and he is God even in the darkness. He is."

"Yes," Kevin replies as he lets out a sigh. "He is."

Chapter 8

A T THE VILLAGE WHERE KARINA AND HER BROTHERS ARE held hostage, Karina finds herself dozing off to sleep, and as she sleeps, she begins to dream. Karina dreams that she's floating on her back in an ocean. As she continues to float, she looks up to the sky and sees clouds and sunshine. A flock of birds flies across her view. Suddenly, she hears a voice calling her name. "Karina." Sitting up, she sees Victor and her four other brothers swimming toward her. "It is a good day, is it not, Karina?" Victor asks as he and the other brothers swim around her.

"It is a good day… a very good day!"

She then sees Kevin and Ruth swimming toward her. "Mother, Father! You are here as well?"

"Why not?" Kevin replies. "We all must enjoy this glorious day!"

"Are you enjoying the day, Karina?" Ruth then asks her.

"I am, Mother," says Karina. "I wish we could have more days like this one."

"We will, Daughter, I promise," Ruth tells her, "but not until the storm passes."

"S-torm?" Karina questions. "What s-s-storm?"

At that moment, dark clouds stretch across the sky, causing Karina to lose sight of her family. The wind begins to fiercely blow, causing the waters to violently rage. Lighting flickers throughout the atmosphere, and shortly thereafter, the sky sends forth a vociferous thunder that shakes the entire earth. Suddenly, heavy rain begins to fall. Karina, now caught in the middle of a storm, cries out, "Fa- fa-Father… Ma-ma-Mother… save me!

Upon rendering a desperate cry, Karina looks and sees…

Her dream is abruptly interrupted when she wakes… due to someone pulling on her feet. Sitting up, she looks and sees two African men putting shackles on them. They then pull Karina out of the cage and fasten her hands together with another set of shackles. After being stood up, Karina asks, "Wh-wh-why are you doing this to uf?" Nonetheless, the men give no reply. "Why… why can't you just leave uf alone," Karina adds as she begins to cry.

The men then chain Karina to a line of other captured African people. Looking in line, she sees an African woman who's chained directly in front of her; in front of the woman are her brothers, with Emmanuel standing in front of the line. As she continues to stare, she realizes they all have thick Y-shaped logs that are resting on their shoulders, with the opening part of the log positioned around their necks. She then notices that Victor is crying heavily. "Don't cry, Victor," Karina shouts to him. "Fa-ther and Mo-ther will find us s-oon and they will s-ave us."

An African man then takes hold of a loose chain that is attached to the end of Emmanuel's log. With an African man in front, two on each side, and one position in the back of the line, they begin to lead Emmanuel and the rest of their prisoners out of the village. As the line begins moving forward, the African man behind Karina pokes her with his spear. "Go, go!" he shouts. "Go!"

Chapter 9

THAT MORNING AT THE LOG CABIN, RUTH ANXIOUSLY PACES the floor. Stopping for a moment, she goes and looks out the front window. There she sees Kevin standing outside, having a conversation with a bishop from the orphanage. As the two men turn and make their way inside, Ruth quickly moves away from the window.

"Ruth," Kevin then says as he and the bishop sorrowfully come inside. "You remember the bishop from the orphanage?"

"I do. Hello, Bishop Amari."

"Hello, Ruth. It's a shame that we are seeing each other under such bad circumstances, and unfortunately, I do have some unpleasant news for you."

"God Almighty, Bishop... what troubling news do you have for me?"

"It grieves my heart to tell you this, but with the slave trade still going on, there is a possibility that your sons and daughter may have been kidnapped by those who chose to participate in the horrific custom. Nonetheless, we will not give up hope. We will keep looking."

"Thank you, Bishop," Ruth lightly says. She then goes toward the kitchen, grabs a stack of dishes off the shelf, and begins setting the table. Kevin and the Bishop look confusedly at each other.

"Thank you, Bishop," Kevin then says as he ushers him to the door. "We will meet up in a little while," he adds as the bishop leaves the house. After closing the front door, Kevin looks at Ruth.

"Ruth?" he then asks, "What are you doing?"

"What does it look like I am doing... I am setting the table for breakfast."

"But you are putting out all the dishes for the entire family?"

"I know?"

"Ruth... Karina and the boys are not here."

"No, they are not here, Kevin," she stops and says as she gloomily looks at the floor. "But they will return," she looks up and says with a smile as she resumes setting the table, "They will come walking through the door any moment now."

"No, Ruth," Kevin says as he slowly walks toward her with tears in his eyes. "No… they are not here, Ruth; they are still lost. We still have to find them, and you heard what the bishop said; they may have even been kidnapped."

"Nonsense… *Nonsense*. They just lost their way in the woods, that is all, and they will find their way back home shortly… just in time for breakfast."

"No, Ruth," says Kevin as he draws closer to her. "No," he adds. Now standing beside her, he lovingly grabs her arm. He then looks her in the eyes and says, "Our children have been kidnapped."

"No," Ruth then shouts as she throws the remaining dishes in her hands onto the floor. "No!" she screams as she pushes the other dishes off the table. "They are coming back… our children are coming back!"

"Ruth, Ruth," Kevin calls as he tries to calm her down. "Ruth," he calls once more as he tightly wraps his arms around her. "Ruth."

Now in his arms, Ruth begins to sob uncontrollably as her knees give way to the floor.

"I know Ruth, I know," says Kevin as he bows with her. "My heart is overwhelmed with grief, too. But even in such a moment like this, God is still God. He is God of the sunshine… Say it with me, Ruth, say it with me." Ruth begins to say it with Kevin. "He is God of the rain. He is God in the light, and he is God even in the darkness. He is."

At that moment, Kevin sees his son Bryan standing there with a fearful look in his eyes. "Come, Bryan," he then tells his son as he extends a hand. The three of them remain on the floor, hold each other close… and cry.

That afternoon, Kevin takes his son Bryan to a nearby field to play kickball. "Are you enjoying yourself?" Kevin asks as he and Bryan kick the ball back and forth.

"Yes, Father, I love playing kickball, but I still wish Victor was here. Where is he?"

Stopping the ball with his foot, Kevin lets out a sigh. "Bryan come here," he then tells him as he sits on the ground and folds his legs. "Come here and sit on my lap."

Bryan goes and sits on his dad's lap, and as Bryan faces forward, his dad tightly wraps his arms around him. He then says to Bryan, "Your sister and your brothers are missing Bryan."

"Where are they?"

"We don't know. That's why we are looking for them, so we can make sure they are safe and bring them home."

"Is that why Mother was very upset earlier?"

"Unfortunately, yes. She misses your sister and your brothers very much, and sometimes when adults miss people, they do odd things."

"I miss them too."

"I know you do, son."

"I wanna help bring them home safe!"

"You do?"

"Yes! What can I do?"

"Well, you can pray. Pray that God will bring them home safely."

"Can we pray right now?"

"Sure, we can pray now."

"Okay then." Closing his eyes, Bryan prays, "Dear God, please bring Victor, Karina, and the rest of my brothers home safe… Amen."

"Amen."

"Father, can I ask you a question?"

"Yes, son."

"You said Mother is very upset, but are you very upset?"

"Yes son, I am."

"Don't be upset, Father. God will bring them back home soon."

"Yeah?"

"Yes!"

"Wow, you are so positive, Bryan… just like your mother."

Beaming with pride, Kevin gives his son a kiss on the cheek, and Bryan kisses his dad in return.

"Alright," says Kevin as he begins standing up. Once up, he faces his back toward Bryan then bends over. "Come on," he then says, "let's head back to the house." Bryan, catching onto his gesture, climbs onto his father's back. Once secure, Kevin begins making his way to the house with Bryan.

Chapter 10

AFTER DAYS OF TRAVELING THROUGH MOUNTAIN TRAILS and dense woods, a tired and dehydrated Karina reaches the coast of Guinea along with the woman and her brothers. Now breathing profusely, she looks down and realizes that her feet are swollen... even bloody. Her legs and arms are covered with sandy dust, and plastered to her sweaty body are tiny insects. As the African men continue to lead Karina and others to the port, she sees in the distance a large white building made out of stone. "Finally, we have arrived," she hears an African man say to another.

Karina sees European officers who are standing at attention at the building's entrance. In front of the officers stands a general. "We are here, General, with the prisoners just as you asked," the African man in front of the line says to him.

With a stern look on his face, the general slowly walks from the head of the line to the back while inspecting each person.

"Dirty," he then says as he walks back to the front of the line, "But still in good condition. Men," the general then says to the soldiers, "Help take these weights off the prisoners' necks, and after that, usher them into the courtyard."

"Yes, Sir," they all answer.

Once the logs are taken off Karina's brothers' shoulders, Karina, the woman, and her brothers are all escorted to an iron gate. A gate that opens to a courtyard. Now inside, the general says, "You men, take the male prisoners to the dungeon over to the left and the women—" But his instructions are cut short when suddenly he hears chains being loosened. Turning toward the sound, he looks wide-eyed when he sees that Emmanuel has managed to loosen the chains that were on his arms.

Now free, Emmanuel positions himself in a stance in which he's ready to pounce.

"Grab him," shouts the general as he watches Emmanuel back away slowly. "Grab him, I say!" The soldiers surround Emmanuel, but seeing an angry-looking, muscular black man who stands much taller than them, they find themselves proceeding with caution.

Suddenly, a soldier comes into the courtyard. Seeing the soldiers trying to capture Emmanuel, he attempts to help by discreetly recapturing Emmanuel from behind.

"E-Emmanuel," Karina then shouts, "Behind you!"

Looking behind, Emmanuel sees the soldier, grabs him, then places him in a choke hold. The other soldiers then bombard Emmanuel and tackle him to the ground.

"Ahhh," Emmanuel screams as he tries to break free but is unable to. The general then makes his way into the chaos. Once there, he pins the side of Emmanuel's face to the ground with his dirty, heavy boot. As his foot remains, he pulls a pistol from his belt and rams it into Emmanuel's temple.

"Do you wish to die, right here, right now... Do you?"

A hostile-looking Emmanuel gives no reply

"Answer me, boy," the general then shouts. "Do you wish to die?"

The question asked causes Emmanuel to look at Karina, who's staring at him with tears in her eyes. "No," he then reluctantly answers, "I do not wish to die."

"Then behave!" the general tells him. "Now stand him up," he says to the soldiers, "and make sure his chains are properly secure this time." Once the soldiers chain Emmanuel's hands behind his back, they stand him to his feet. "Now take the men to their dungeon and the women to theirs!"

Moments later, Karina finds herself being led down a dark hallway that travels downward to a dark room. As she continues to descend, an indescribable stench greets her, a stench so strong that it begins burning her nostrils. As she descends even further, she can hear screams and cries echoing from below. Now in the dungeon's belly, she sees a silhouette of narrow doorways with gates in front of them. The screams and cries that are now bursting her eardrums are pinpointed as she realizes they are coming from behind the gates. Officers then lead Karina and the other woman to one of the gates, and as he opens the gate, he says while smiling, "Welcome, ladies, to the door of no return. Whatever life you had here in Africa... has now come to an end."

"No, no... not so," Karina thinks to herself. "I will return... Father and Mother will find me and rescue me. Once the gate is open, Karina and the other woman are forced inside.

Once inside...

Chapter 11

KARINA'S FEET ARE GREETED WITH A SQUISHY, liquid substance. A tiny ray of light that comes from a small window inside the cell serves as an advocate for her to be able to look down and see what she is standing on. However, the ray of light that once served as assistance now betrays her when she looks down and realizes that she's now standing in a puddle that's filled with blood, saliva, urine, and human feces. Suddenly, Karina feels something fall on her shoulder. Turning to see what it might be, she realizes that a dead body has just fallen on her. *"God Almighty!"* she then says as she maneuvers backward so the body can fall away. A sudden squeaking sound from down below causes her to look to the floor once more, and there she sees rats crawling between her and the other women's legs.

"Oh fa-fa-Father," she then cries out, "Come quick and s-ave me! Sa-sa- save me, Father! Sa-sa- save me!" She manages to maneuver her way through the crowd until she reaches a stone wall. Once at the wall, she moves into a corner and leans. Her exhaustion then causes her to drift off to sleep, and as she sleeps… she dreams the same dream she dreamed earlier.

Karina dreams she is floating on her back in an ocean. As she continues to float, she looks up to the sky and sees clouds and sunshine. "Karina." She suddenly hears a voice calling her name. Sitting up, she sees Victor and her four other brothers swimming toward her. "It is a good day, is it not, Karina?" Victor asks as he and the other brothers swim around her.

"It is a good day… a very good day!"

She then sees Kevin and Ruth swimming towards her, "Mother, Father! You are here as well?"

"Why not?" Kevin replies, "We all must enjoy this day!"

"Are you enjoying the day, Karina?" Ruth then asks her

"I am, Mother," says Karina, "I wish we could have more days like this one."

"We will, I promise," Ruth tells her, "But not until the storm passes."

"*Storm?*" Karina questions, "What s-s-storm?"

At that moment, dark clouds stretch across the sky, causing Karina to lose sight of her family. The wind begins to fiercely blow, causing the waters to rage. Lighting flickers throughout the atmosphere, and shortly thereafter, the sky sends forth a vociferous thunder that shakes the entire earth. Suddenly, heavy rain begins to fall. Karina, now caught in the middle of a storm, cries out, "Fa-fa- Father… Ma-Mother… sa- sa- save me!

Upon rendering a desperate cry, Karina looks and sees… a boat and station inside the boat…is a paddle. She is then woken by the sound of…

Chapter 12

THE IRON GATE BEING OPENED. SOLDIERS THEN come inside the cell and hastily begin moving her and the other females out of the cell and to a large metal door. The door is then opened, and Karina sees that it's an early foggy morning. Looking a few feet ahead, she sees a number of boats stationed at the shore. Her attention is then directed out at sea to a large ship adorned with white flags.

Once taken to shore, Karina is manhandled into one of the boats. As the boat begins pulling away, Karina feels her heart beginning to sink. "Is it so," Karina thinks to herself, "Is thif really happening? I so-so desperately wanted to believe that all of thif waf just a bad dream in-stead it haf become a cruel reality."

As the boat continues to pull away, Karina finds herself thinking back to her life in Africa. She recalls the time as a little girl when she stood in the center of her village and looked at the creatively painted huts. She recalls watching everyone in the village as they did their share of work and the joyful celebrations they had as a tribe.

She remembers her birth mother (Ozigbodi) extending her arms toward her while smiling. She remembers sitting on her birth daddy's (Donkor) lap and watching the nightly stars. She recalls the exuberant feeling she felt with her birth brothers when they picked her up and swung her around.

As she continues to think back to such times, she remembers the moments when she sat at the table with Ruth, Kevin, and her other brothers, laughing while eating a meal.

As she now watches Africa slowly disappear into the thick morning fog, she says with tears in her eyes… Africa… my home… no more.

She then looks to the floor of the boat and sobs.

Moments later, Karina arrives on board the ship. Once there, she is taken to the belly of the vessel. Now standing at the ship's bottom, Karina watches as soldiers aggressively grab other African females, lay them down on the ship's floor, then fasten them together with thick chains. As she continues to witness the sight, Karina looks and sees the tall, dark skin man in the white robe standing a few feet away, and as he stands there, he sorrowfully looks at her.

Suddenly, Karina is grabbed. She is laid down and shackled to the other women. Once the men finish fastening Karina and the other women to the floor, a man looks at a man who's standing near the basement doorway and tells him, "We're done down here and ready to go."

"Alright," the man replies, "I will let the captain know." He then turns and goes up above.

Before long, Karina feels the ship beginning to move. She's confused and scared about what is going on. However, the rocking back and forth motion of the ship causes her to doze off to sleep, and as she sleeps, she dreams once more. For the third time, Karina dreams that she's swimming in the ocean. As her family swims around her, her mother asks, "Are you enjoying the day?"

"I am, Mother," Karina responds, "I wish we could have more days like this one."

"We will, I promise," Ruth tells her, "But not until the storm passes."

"*Storm?*" Karina questions, "What s-s-storm?"

At that moment, dark clouds stretch across the sky, causing Karina to lose sight of her family. The wind begins to fiercely blow, causing the waters to rage. Lighting flickers throughout the atmosphere, and shortly thereafter, the sky sends forth a vociferous thunder that shakes the entire earth. Suddenly, heavy rain begins to fall. Karina, now caught in the middle of a storm, cries out, "Fa-fa- father... Ma- mother...sumbody...anybody...sa- sa save me...save me plea-se!"

Upon rendering her desperate cry, Karina looks and sees... a boat... with a paddle inside. She swims towards the boat and gets inside. Once there, she looks at the storm happening around her. "How will I get through thif?" she says as she continues to look around, "There is no one here to save me... no one."

"Use the paddle," she suddenly hears a voice say from behind. Turning toward the voice, she sees...

Suddenly, Karina is awakened by the sound of thundering coming from up above and outside the ship. Inhaling then exhaling, she goes back to sleep and once again... she dreams she's sitting in the boat. As she sits there, she looks at the storm happening around her. "How will I get through thif?" she says as she continues to look around. "There is no one here to s-ave me... no one."

"Use the paddle," she suddenly hears a voice say from behind. Turning toward the voice... Karina sees the tall man with a white robe and dark skin sitting at the back of the boat.

"Who are you?" she asks him, "And why do I keep s-eeing you?"

"My name is Abaven... I'm an angel, your guardian angel, and I've been sent by God to help you. But you must make a choice."

"A choice? What choice can I make in the mif of all of thif? I cannot control the storm!"

"No, you cannot. But what you can control is whether or not you get through the storm and even how the storm will affect you. So, again I say, use the paddle."

"But why the pad-dle... why even the b-oat? Can't God just deliver me from thif? Or can't he just s-end my father or my mother to res-cue me?"

"Karina, remember your mother's words. Sometimes, God will move troubled waters out of our way like he did for Moses and the children of Israel. And sometimes, God will allow us to rise above and walk on those troubled waters like he did for Peter when he was out at sea. But then there are times when God will just make sure we have a paddle and a boat. He won't move problems out of our way nor will he cause us to rise above them. Sometimes, God will simply give us the strength we need to endure. So, with that being said, what will you choose to do... what will you do? Will you use the paddle... will you?" Upon hearing Abaven's words, Karina looks at the paddle to ponder the thought.

She is then awakened by dripping water on her face, water that is coming from the deck up above. She tries to turn to escape the trickling, but due to being strapped to the floor so tightly, she is unable to escape the drenching. She then sees men coming from up above. Once there, they begin unstrapping her and the other females. "Oh, thank heavens," Karina lowly says

She and the other prisoners are then escorted to the upper deck. With the boat now stationed at sea, Karina and the other women stand outside on the ship's deck. Karina then sees the soldiers inspecting the other female prisoners, but due to the fact that she didn't sleep well, she finds herself nodding off.

"No!" She is then startled when she hears a woman screaming. Karina sees two men pulling a sickly-looking woman from the line to the deck's edge. Once there, they lift her up... and toss her overboard. Looking on with fear, Karina begins to tremble and, overwhelmed by what she just saw, she turns her head to the side and vomits.

One of the men who witnessed Karina's spews walks up to her. He looks at Karina and then at what she had ejected. He then unchains her from the line and begins pulling her to the ship's edge. "No... no," Karina begins to say in disbelief. "No!" She then screams as she finds herself being pulled closer to the ship's edge, "No... do not tof me into the water... I'm not si-si-sick... I'm not s-ick!" With only inches away from the edge, the man prepares to throw Karina overboard. However, just before doing so, the captain yells.

"John!"

"Yes, Captain," he stops and answers.

"Put her back!"

At the request of the captain, the man returns Karina to the line. With her heart feeling as though it's about to burst through her chest, Karina inhales and then exhales.

Chapter 13

TWO DAYS PRIOR, ON AN EARLY FOGGY MORNING, SISTER Patricia (a caretaker for the orphanage and a woman who became a close friend of the family) kneels on the veranda of the orphanage building, and as she does, she engages in her routine morning prayers. "Dear heavenly Father, as I begin my day, I pray that you will be with me. Guide me, heavenly Father. May my eyes be open to see what you need me to see… in your name, amen."

Standing to her feet, she begins to make her way inside when suddenly her attention is drawn to a sight in the distance. Looking, she sees African people being taken from Elmina Castle and loaded into a boat. Sighing and shaking her head, she says out loud, "Dear Lord, when will this terrible slave trade end?" She begins turning away but stops and looks back at the sight, and as she continues to stare, her eyes begin to open wide. "No," she then says with her voice barely ghosting between her lips. "No, it can't be… no!" she says as she begins to sob. "No!"

An hour later, Sister Patricia sits outside of the cabin and talks to Kevin. "I am so sorry, Kevin," she tells him with tears streaming down her face. "So, so, sorry. I wish there was something I could do."

"Maybe there is," Kevin tells her with his eyes fixated on the group.

Moments later, a gloomy-looking Kevin enters the house, and as he enters, he sees Ruth sitting by the fireplace, aimlessly staring at the fire. She holds in her hand a silver necklace with the Star of David attached to it. She turns, takes one look at Kevin, then resumes watching the fire. "I heard her," she then says to Kevin while still staring into the fire. "I heard what Sister Patricia told you… So, it is true after all… our children have been kidnapped."

"Yes," Kevin lightly answers, "they have. Sister Patricia saw a number of African prisoners being taken from Elmina Castle and loaded into the boats. Among those prisoners was Karina, and more than likely the boys too."

"So, I guess that is it," Ruth despondently says. "Our children are gone... gone."

"No, Ruth, no," says Kevin as he suddenly draws from the door and sits on a stool in front of her. "That is *not* it. We can find the children and bring them back home. Ships leave the port nearly every day. We can board a ship to South Carolina and look for them there."

"And what will we do, Kevin, if we happen to find them there?" She then looks at him and says with an aggravated look on her face. "Those who hold them captive will not let us have our children back... they are their prisoners now. They own them."

"Then I will fight the men who own them!"

"And even if you do fight them and win, where would we even begin to look? Those ships don't just travel to South Carolina; they travel all over the world. Our children could be anywhere. I love you, Kevin... I do. I love you, but your head is stuck in the clouds. What you are saying is foolish... just plain foolish." Upon rendering such words, Ruth resumes looking into the fire. Kevin, still seated, stares at her as she continues to stare into the fire.

Kevin looks to the floor and sighs. "Maybe you are right," Kevin then says. "Maybe I am being foolish." Jumping to his feet, he makes his way toward the kitchen table but stops when he sees something sitting on the shelf above the stove. Ruth's attention towards the fire is then interrupted when she sees a jar of salt and a jar of sugar placed on the stool in front of her. Kevin then takes a seat on the floor next to the stool, and as Ruth continues to stare at the jars, she hears Kevin say...

"I remember one time there was this woman who believed that all things were possible, even teaching a little African girl the difference between right and wrong. But there was this man, who shall remain nameless, who did not believe in *anything*. So, when he saw this woman trying to teach this little girl, a little girl who could not only speak English but a little girl who could *not* even speak at all... Well, he thought that the woman was just being foolish; he thought that the woman's head was stuck in the clouds. But regardless of what the man thought, the woman went on to teach this little girl anyway, using this jar of salt and this jar of sugar. And not only did the little African girl understand what was being taught to her, but she even uttered her very first word. All because the woman believed that all things were possible." As Ruth hears Kevin's words and stares at the jars, tears begin to well up in her eyes.

"Wait a minute!" she then says.

"What?"

"Okay, who are you, and what have you done with my husband? You know, Mr. Pessimistic. The man who always shook his head and rolled his eyes whenever I tried to do something positive. The man who told me how impossible something was. Where's that man... Have you seen him?"

"Well, maybe after all these years, you rubbed off on me."

Shaking her head, she then rolls her eyes and looks away.

"Ruth," Kevin then says as he kneels beside her, "I know what I am suggesting might seem like a long shot, but we have to try. We can start in South Carolina, a place where ships not only dock but a place that is also our home. Our family is there. They miss us; they write us nearly every day. We can start there, and while we are looking, be with family who can give us all the love and support that we could really use right now. We have to try Ruth... we have to... we owe it to the children to do so."

"And what about the child we still have here, Kevin? What about Bryan? How will he handle all of this? Does he even know what's going on?"

"He knows; I talked to him."

"You did... Well, how did he take it?"

"A lot better than I thought. He's a strong kid, Ruth. A kid who's full of hope... just like his mother. He even asked what he could do to help!"

"He did?"

"Yes."

"Hum, he is strong. Even in the midst of darkness, he has the courage to be the light... just like his father." For a second, Ruth closes her eyes and sighs. She then opens them, looks at Kevin, and says, "Okay, let's do it... Let's go to South Carolina."

"I love you, Ruth Hopkins," says Kevin as he embraces her.

"I love you too," says Ruth as he hugs him in return.

As they withdraw from each other's embrace, Kevin looks down and sees the silver necklace in Ruth's hand.

"The silver necklace you gave Karina. You still have it?"

"I do. I found it in her room this morning. Karina never liked wearing the necklace when she walked in the woods; she was afraid it might get lost or broken."

Kevin then places his hands inside Ruth's. "One day Karina will wear this necklace again... I believe it."

"Yes, she will."

Chapter 14

TWO DAYS LATER, KEVIN, RUTH, AND BRYAN ARRIVE AT THE port of Guinea. As Bryan walks beside his parents, he carries in his arms a brown rubber ball. Kevin, seeing a man standing at a dock, approaches him and asks, "We're looking for the steamship to America!?"

"This is it," the man tells him

"How long is the voyage?" Ruth asks

"About fifteen days."

"And how much for me, my wife, and the boy?"

"All together... 200."

"200?" says Kevin with wide eyes. "We were told thirty dollars apiece, and my son shouldn't even be full price since he's just a boy. Can you please assist us? We are going to America to find the rest of our children."

"I cannot."

"You can't, or you won't?" Kevin angrily says

As Bryan watches his father argue with the dock attendant, the ball slips out of his hands. Now on the ground, the ball begins rolling away. Bryan follows behind to retrieve it, but suddenly the ball is stopped by the foot of a thin and frail-looking man with pasty skin. Picking up the ball, he looks at Bryan and asks with a sketchy tone, "Is this your ball, little boy?"

Bryan, looking at the man with glazed eyes, slowly nods his head. "Yes."

"Want it back?"

"Yes," Bryan lightly answers.

"Ok then... come over here and get it," says the man as he extends his arm with the ball firmly grasped in the palm of his hand.

Bryan slowly walks toward the man to get his ball. Once there, he nearly grabs it when the man quickly moves it away. He then extends his arm toward Bryan once more. Bryan tries to grab the ball again, but again the man quickly moves it away.

"Hey!" The man then hears another man shout. Looking, he sees a raging Kevin running toward him. "Leave him alone... leave my child alone! I won't let you hurt him," Kevin screams as he gets in the man's face. "You hear me... I won't let you." With a screaming Kevin now in the man's face, the man quickly gives Bryan back the ball. "Yeah, you better give him back his ball... now get lost!" The man turns and quickly runs away.

As Kevin watches the man run away, Ruth approaches him from behind. "Bryan, are you okay?" she looks at him and asks.

Bryan, now with a ball in his hands, nods his head. "Yes."

"Are you okay?" she then asks Kevin as she sees him still looking away with an angry look on his face. "Kevin?" she calls again, but still he doesn't answer, nor does he look her way. "Kevin?" she calls once more, but still he gives no reply.

"I was supposed to protect them, Ruth," he then says while still looking away. "I was supposed to protect our children... that's my job...to protect my family. But I didn't... I couldn't. What kind of man am I?"

"A good one," Ruth replies as she steps into Kevin's view. As she lovingly places both arms around his shoulder, she adds, "You are a good husband... a good father... a good man. Never doubt that." Kevin, now looking at her, gives her a kiss on the lips. "Come on," Ruth then says, "Let's head back to the dock."

"And pay $200," Kevin tells her.

"No, $80. I talked him down."

"Hum, I love you, Ruth Hopkins."

"I love you, too, Kevin Hopkins."

They begin to turn and walk away, but suddenly Ruth stops, looks at Bryan, and says, "Bryan... did that man touch your kickball?"

"Yes," he lightly answers.

"That man looks like he was sick," she whispers to Kevin.

"Bryan, maybe you should just leave the ball here," Kevin tells him.

"No!" Bryan shouts. "This is Victor's kickball, and I want to give it to him when I see him again."

Upon hearing Bryan's words, Kevin and Ruth look at each other with teary eyes and a smile.

"Okay, Bryan," Ruth then says. "You can bring the ball, but just stay close to us."

"Please!" Kevin adds.

As the three of them begin to make their way to the loading dock, Ruth says aloud, "My oh my, our time here in Africa has been such an experience."

"Do I sense regret in your voice?" Kevin asks.

"No, my love… no regret. Life is a journey, no matter where I go. I am eternally grateful that I am able to take this journey with you. I love you, Kevin."

"I love you, too, Ruth."

Chapter 15

DAYS LATER, THE VESSEL ON WHICH KARINA IS HELD hostage finally reaches land.

As she is escorted off the ship, she sees a wooden sign that reads "South Carolina."

She is then taken to a stone building that resembles a barn. The floors are muddy and covered with hay, and there are small individual areas enclosed with black iron gates.

Once forced inside one of the areas, Karina sees a gated window. Moving quickly toward the window, she looks outside and sees a host of people standing before a well-elevated wooden stage with small wooden paddles in their hands. As she continues to stare, she sees an African man being brought onto the stage by a soldier. With shackles still around his neck, hands, and feet, he stands with a look of fear and confusion on his face. Suddenly, an elderly Caucasian man approaches the stage and stands beside the African man. Displaying a funny-shaped hat on his head, he is wearing a white puffy shirt, a brown vest, and brown pants that extend tightly just beyond his knees.

The Caucasian man then begins to talk to the crowd very quickly. However, Karina is able to make out the words. Karina hears the Caucasian man say, "We have here today one male negro; he stands at six foot and a three; he is young, he is heathy and he is strong. He would make a good field slave or a house slave: whatsoever you so choose. Shall we start the bidding at $1,600?"

Upon the auctioneer asking the question, Karina sees a Caucasian man in the crowd raise a paddle while saying, "$1,600!"

"We have $1,600 from the gentleman in front. Do I hear $1,650?"

"$1,650!" Karina sees another Caucasian man in the crowd say as he raises his paddle.

"We have $1,650 from the gentleman over to my left. Do I hear $1,700?"

"$1,700!" says a Caucasian man standing in the center.

"$1,700 from the gentleman standing in the center. Do I hear $1,750?" The crowd is silent. "$1,700 going once; $1,700 going twice... sold! To the gentleman standing in the center."

Once the Caucasian man on the stage has yelled, "Sold," the African man is taken off stage. Turning away from the window, Karina presses her back against the wall. "What... what... what is going on here... what are they going to do to uf?"

"They are buying us so they can take us to their land and work us as slaves," Karina suddenly hears a female voice say. Looking past the iron bars, Karina sees an African woman close to her age in a cage on the other side.

"How do you know thif?" Karina asks as she draws near to the bars.

"I overheard the soldiers talking, saying what a good batch of prisoners they have this time and how much money will be made once the prisoners are sold to plantation owners and used as their slaves."

"No... no," Karina begins to say as she shakes her head with tears in her eyes, "No!" she shouts as she backs away from the bars and returns to the window. "Oh, dear God," Karina says while looking out the window, "Let, let it not be true." Suddenly, she sees Victor being ushered onto the stage. With chains still around his neck, hands, and feet, he cries uncontrollably. "Victor!" Karina shouts. "Do... do not cry! Fa-ther will find us and save us so-oon!" However, Victor is not able to hear her.

The auctioneer then stands besides Victor and begins to say, "We have here today another male negro; he stands at five foot and a seven; he too is young, healthy, and strong. He would make a good field slave or a house slave: whatsoever you so choose. Shall we start the bidding at $1,300?"

Karina sees a Caucasian man in the crowd raise a paddle.

"We have $1,300 from my right. Do I hear $1,350?"

"$1,350!" she hears another Caucasian man in the crowd say as he raises his paddle.

"We have $1,350 from another gentleman over to my right. Do I hear $1,400?"

"$1,400!" says a Caucasian man standing in the center.

"1,400 from the man in the center. Do I hear $1,450?"

"$1,500!" suddenly says a Caucasian man standing in the back of the crowd.

"$1,500 from the gentleman in the back. Do I hear $1,550?... $1,500 going once; $1,500 going twice; sold! To the gentleman in the back."

Karina then sees a tearful Victor being ushered off stage, and Karina cries out, "Victor!" Turning away from the window, she squats to the floor, buries her face into her knees, and sobs.

"Abena," she suddenly hears a female voice call,

"Abena?" she lightly questions as she raises her head up from her lap. "Haven't heard that name in a very long time… that's my birth name. Mama," she calls out, "are you here?"

"I am," says her birth mother, Ozigbodi.

Karina sees Ozigbodi standing in the corner of the cage.

"Mama," Karina says as she looks at her sorrowful eyes. "Oh Mama," Karina then says as tears begin to pour out of her eyes. "So, so much evil has happened… to you… to me… *to all* our people. We have been taken away from our land, our ho-mes and even from our fam-mi-lies, and now, we are about to be turned into… sa- sa- slaves."

After hearing her daughter's groan, Ozigbodi walks closer. Once there, she stoops down in front of her, places her fingers on Karina's chin, then says,

"Oh, my dear child…You might think being brought to this country, under these circumstances, is a catastrophe. But let me assure you, what the enemy means for bad, God *will* turn it around and make it work for good… You will see!"

"Oh, but Mama," Karina sobs, "I'm all alone."

"*Abena,*" says Ozigbodi, "You are not alone… look!"

Karina sees, standing behind her, her birth father, Donkor, and her thirteen birth brothers. As Karina witnesses the sight, she stands to her feet. "Papa… brothers," she then says as she looks at them with awe. "You are here! You are all here!"

"We never left," Donkor tells her. "We are with you wherever you go. Remember that, my daughter, when days are long and nights are cold. Re-member… we are with you!"

Suddenly…

Chapter 16

TWO SOLDIERS ENTER THE CAGE. ONCE THERE, they forcibly escort Karina out of the cage. She is then taken outside and taken onto the stage, and as she stands there, the Caucasian man stands beside her then says, "We have here today a female negro; she stands at five foot and a seven; she is young, heathy, and strong. She looks as though she would make a good house slave, but because she is so dark and somewhat ugly, you might want to keep her in the field. Shall we start the bidding at $1,000?"

"$1,000," says a Caucasian man as he raises his paddle. Sporting salt and pepper hair and a beard, he wears a green velvet petticoat.

"We have $1,000 from the gentleman in the center of the crowd. Do I hear $1,050?"

"$1,050!" says another Caucasian man standing in the back.

"$1,050 to the gentleman in the back," says the auctioneer. "Do I hear "$1,100?... $1,100 going once; $1,100 going twice..."

As the Caucasian man in the green petticoat listens to the auctioneer's bidding, he stares oddly at Karina. "$2,000!" he then shouts as he raises his paddle. Upon his shouting out such a price, people in the crowd gasp.

The auctioneer, now looking at him wide-eyed, says, "$2,000 from the man in the green petticoat. Such an offer for a dark-skinned slave girl. Do I dare hear $2,050?" No one bids. "$2,000 going once; $2,000 going twice. Sold to the man in the green petticoat. And what is your name, sir?" the auctioneer then asks.

"Ehmerney," he says. "My name is Richard Ehmerney."

"Well, Mr. Ehmerney," the auctioneer then says, "you may come to the side of the platform to retrieve your slave."

Once Karina is at the side of the platform, she sees Ehmerney and a younger Caucasian man approaching her. Ehmerney, now standing before Karina, looks her up and down. "Johnathan," Ehmerney then says, "I have papers to fill out. Put this girl in the back of the wagon with the others and make sure you securely fasten her so she doesn't run away. I paid an awful lot for this slave!"

"Yes, Father," Johnathan answers.

As Johnathan leads Karina away, Ehmerney stares intensely at her, and then for a moment, he looks to the ground in deep thought. Raising his head back up, he looks at Karina once more and walks away.

Near the wagon, Karina sees a cart that is painted black and enclosed with mental bars. Sitting inside is a young African man and a woman who happens to be asleep. Opening the cage, Johnathan harshly puts Karina inside; he then locks the gate and walks away.

Now inside the cage, Karina pulls her knees close to her chest. She then rests a hand on top of her legs, looks to the floor, and deeply sighs. As she continues to gaze down at the floor, her eyes come across a person who's wearing gold sandals. Her eyes follow upward and see that the gold sandals belong to the tall, dark skin man in the white robe who happens to be sitting across from her.

"You?" Karina says as she looks at him with wide eyes. "You are the man I s-aw sit-ting on a rock when I w-as a just little girl in my village. You are the man I s-aw just before I en-tered the fo-rest and again ju-st before I got shot by the dart. I sa- sa saw you on the s-hip and even in my drea-ms... Your name... is... A-ba-ven."

"Yes, that is my name... and you are... Karina."

"Yes," she softly answers. "In my dream, you told me that you were my guardian angel... Is that true?"

"It is." Abaven answers. "May I sit beside you, Karina?"

For a second, Karina stares aimlessly at him without saying a word. "Yes," she then lightly answers.

Upon receiving her permission, Abaven moves to where Karina is sitting and sits beside her. Once there, he sees that Karina has a hand resting on her knee. Abaven takes his hand and gently rests it on top of hers. For a moment, Karina looks at Abaven's hand sitting on top of hers, and she then looks at him and realizes that he's now looking at her with a smile. As Karina gazes into Abaven's eyes, a warm and loving sensation covers her from head to toe. Lightly smiling, she then rests her head on Abaven's chest. Abaven wraps his arms around her. Karina, now in Abaven's embrace, hears him whisper, "What you are experiencing right now is a lot, Karina... an awful lot. But even in the midst of all this... God... is still... God. He is God of the sunshine." Karina joins in and begins to say, "He is God of the rain... he is God in the light, and he is God even in the darkness... he is."

As Abaven continues to hold Karina close, she dozes off to sleep, and as she sleeps, she dreams. Karina dreams that she's swimming in the ocean in the middle of a storm. The sky is completely dark, and the raging waters that are being blown by the fierce wind are smacking her in the face. "Fa-Father... Mother," Karina cries out, "hel-hel-help me!"

Upon rendering her desperate cry, Karina looks and sees... a boat with a paddle inside. She swims toward the boat and gets inside. Once there, she looks at the storm. "How will I get through thif?" she says as she continues to look around. "There is no one here to s-s-save me... no one."

"Use the paddle," she suddenly hears a voice say from behind. Turning toward the voice, Karina sees Abaven sitting in the back.

"But why the pad-dle... why even the bo-at? Can't God just deliver me from thif? Or can't he just s-end my father like before to res-cue me s-o that I do not drown?"

"Like your mother once said... Sometimes, God will move troubled waters out of our way like he did for Moses and the children of Israel. And sometimes, God will allow us to rise above and walk on those troubled waters like he did for Peter when he was out at sea. But then there are times when God will just make sure we have a paddle and a boat. He won't move problems out of our way, nor will he cause us to rise above them. Sometimes, God will simply give us the strength we need to endure. So, with that being said, what will you choose to do, Karina? Will you use the paddle... will you? I will even help you if you so choose," Abaven tells her as he picks up a paddle as well. Upon hearing Abaven's words, Karina looks at the paddle to ponder the thought. She then places the paddle into the water... and begins to row.

Seconds later, Karina wakes to the sight of...

Chapter 17

THE WAGON TRAVELING THROUGH A DENSE wooded area. once out of the area, she sees a sign that reads "Camden, South Carolina."

Now riding through a town, Karina sees two-story wooden buildings on both sides of the road. Coming in and out of these buildings are Caucasian men and women. The women are dressed in colorful flared-out dresses that reach to the bottom of their feet. She then notices that the men are wearing long-sleeved ivory shirts with dark brown suit jackets and pants with loose bow ties around their necks. As the wagon continues to make its way through town, Karina sees Caucasian and African men who are either riding horses or operating wagons.

The wagon that Karina is in then rides through open fields. She sees fields that are located on both sides of the wagon, filled with plants that have white cotton balls attached to them. Picking the balls off these plants are African men, women, and even children. She then notices that stationed behind these fields are white two-story houses, each with a porch, a roof, and white pillars.

Suddenly, the wagon makes a left turn and rides up to the last white house on the road. As the wagon approaches the front of the house, Karina sees a two-story white house that's very similar to the others. However, this house has long, white-painted stairs leading to a porch that wraps around the entire house. Holding up the porch's roof are white columns that are positioned in all four corners. Karina, still staring, notices that each window of the house is adorned with black shutters. The wagon then makes its way to an old barn. Once there, the wagon comes to a complete stop. Ehmerney, in the driver's seat, says to Johnathan, in the passenger's seat, "Go inside and let your mother know we're here while I get the slaves out of the wagon."

"Yes, Father."

As Johnathan goes inside, Ehmerney opens and cage and shouts to the African man and woman who are still sleeping… *"Wake up!"* Startled by the sudden call, they quickly sit up.

"There are rules to this plantation here," Ehmerney then says to the three of them in an authoritative voice, "First rule is if you try to leave this plantation, you will be found and severely punished. So, whatever you do, don't make the mistake of running away. Not if you value your life. Now that we got that rule out of the way, I want you to come from inside the wagon and stand in front of the barn." After Karina and the African man and woman step out of the caged wagon, they stand in front of the barn. Ehmerney slowly walks back and forth in front of them. With his hand behind his back, he says, "Second thing to remember about this plantation is that you belong here now. This is your new home, and I... own you. So, when you address me, you will address me as master, and whenever I call you or ask you a question, you will answer, 'Yes, Master.' Do I make myself clear?"

"Yes, Master," Karina and the other two lightly say.

"I can't hear you... Say it louder!"

"Yes, Master."

"Peter... Sarah!" Ehmerney then shouts.

Upon his calling comes an up in aged African man and woman running from nearby. Both have dark complexions and salt and pepper hair. Sarah's hair, coarse but long, is tied backwards and placed into a bun at the base of her head, while Peter sports a mini salt and pepper afro with a salt and pepper mustache and beard.

"Yes, Master," they both answer with a smile.

"Now you see how they ran when I called them?" Ehmerney looks at Karina and the others and says, "And they're even smiling... that's how I expect you to be."

Ehmerney then looks back at the up in aged African man and woman and says, "Sarah, take the women and get them cleaned, clothed, and ready for work. Peter, you do the same with the man."

Upon receiving their command, Sarah and Peter take Karina and the two others to an area where there are a host of small cabins. "Who sleeps in the cabins?" Karina asks as she stares.

"We do," Peter tells her with a laugh.

At the house, Ehmerney arrives in the kitchen through the back door. Once inside, he sees a perturbed-looking Caucasian woman with her hands on her hips. Wearing a long blue puffy dress, she has dark hair that's parted in the center, and in the back are loose, pinned-up curls that cascade past her shoulders.

"Hello, Martha dear," Ehmerney draws close to kiss her, but she quickly turns away.

"$2,000?" Martha then says, "You spend $2,000 on a slave?"

"My, Martha, I wonder who told you that?" Ehmerney says as he looks at his son, who's standing in the corner of the kitchen. Once his son realizes his father is eying him, he quickly looks away.

"I thought we agreed we wasn't going to spend that much on field help."

"Well, plans change," Ehmerney tells her

"Oh, they do, huh? That female slave you spent $2,000 on... betta be worth it."

Martha then hastily leaves the kitchen, and once she has departed, Ehmerney looks to the floor and whispers, "I believe she is."

Chapter 18

INSIDE ONE OF THE CABINS SITS KARINA IN A WOODEN CHAIR. clothed in an off-white shirt and a mismatched dress that extends to her feet, she sits in a chair while Sarah combs her hair.

"My goodness, child," Sarah says with a country accent, "what long, thick hair you have; it's bootiful."

"Thank you."

"Working here on this plantation can not only take a toll on your body, but it can also wreak havoc on your hair, so you must protect it." After placing Karina's hair into a pony tail and braiding it, Sarah grabs a brown sugar-colored scarf from off the kitchen table she then says, "I'm gonna wrap your head in this here scarf so it can be safe, and you wear this scarf on your head every day, you hear?"

"Yes, Ms... what's your name again?"

"Sarah, baby, my name is Sarah... and your name is?"

"Karina."

"What a bootiful name, but you may not have that name for long. One thing that happens when you come to this plantation is that Master will give you a new name?"

"He doef?"

"Yeah, he does."

"So, S-arah is not your original name?"

"No, baby."

"Well, what was your original name?"

"Honestly... I don't remember... It's been so long."

"How long have you been here?"

"Let's see, I came here when I was just nineteen years old, and now I'm..." She begins counting on her fingers. "I've been here..." she continues counting. "No, it's... Oh shoot." She then finally says, "Let's just say I've been here a very long time."

"Ms. Sar-ah?"

"Yes, baby?"

"How do you feel about being here?"

"Well, it was hard at first, but after a while you get used to it."

"Hopefully, I wi-ll not get used to it. Hopefully, I -I will not be he-re too much longer."

"Oh Karina," she shakes her head and laughs. "Don't you go getting ideas. Master don't like it when slaves get ideas."

Just then, a knock is heard at the cabin door.

Sarah opens it and sees Peter standing there.

"Sarah," he says with a country accent, "Master says he wants to see the new slaves, and he wants to see them... *now*."

"Yes'um, Peter, wesa coming right now. Come, Karina," She then walks towards her and grabs her hand. "Master wants to see us now, and when he calls, we musta come running."

Moments later, at the barn, Karina and the others stand before Master Ehmerney while Sarah and Peter stand off to the side. Ehmerney once more paces back and forth. With his hands behind his back, he looks toward the sky and says, "As I mentioned before, this is your new home now. You belong to me, and you will do as you are told. Do you hear me?"

"Yes, Master," they all answer.

"I paid a good price for you... some more than others," he adds as he stops and looks at Karina. "So," he says as he resumes pacing, "I want to get my money's worth."

Ehmerney then walks up to the male slave. Looking at him, he sees a very young African man of dark complexion. As Ehmerney stands before him, he trembles with fear.

"Are you scared?" Ehmerney asks him with a laugh.

The young African man opens his mouth to answer but begins to stutter, "Na, na, no... Mas... ter."

Laughing, Ehmerney mockingly repeats, "Na, na... no." He then asks, "So, what's your name, boy?"

"Ah... Ah, Adusa," he answers, "My-name is A-dusa

"Ad what,"

"Ah... Ah..." he stutters.

"Oh, for heaven's sakes, forget it! Your name is now Freddy. Got it?"

"Yes...yes... Ma... ster," the young man struggles to answer, but Ehmerney stops him by placing a hand over his mouth.

"Just nod your head yes."

With Ehmerney's hand still over his mouth, the young man simply nods his head yes.

Ehmerney then approaches a young African female of dark complexion and sees that she has taken the liberty to stoop down on the ground.

"What are you doing?" Ehmerney shouts. "Stand up!"

"I'm tired of standing," the young African girl replies.

"Is that right?" Ehmerney says as he places his hands on his hips. "Well, maybe... a good whipping will help!"

"Never mind, I'll stand up."

Once she is up, Ehmerney asks, "And what is your name?"

"Sisi."

"What... what kind of name is that? From now on, your name is going to be Lisa. Do you hear me?"

"Yes, Master," she answers.

Ehmerney then approaches Karina. Once in front of her, he looks her up and down. "And what's your name?" he asks.

"Hello, my name is Karina," she says with a smile.

"My name is Karina," Ehmerney repeats in a mocking tone. "Well, I don't like that name, so I'm gonna call you..." He pauses and looks to the ground. "Denise," he then looks at her and says. "Yeah, that's your new name now. Denise... got it?"

"Yes," Karina answers with glazed eyes

"Yes, what?" Ehmerney says as he places his hands on his hips.

"Yes, Maf-ter."

"Maf-ter? Maf-ter? That's not how you say that word; it's *Mas-ter*! Say it."

"Maf-ter."

"No!" he says as he huffs and puffs, getting in her face. "It's Mas-ter!"

"Maf-ter."

"Say *Mas...*"

"Mas."

"*Terrr.*"

"Terrr."

"Now put it together and say it."

"...Maf-ter."

After hearing Karina mispronounce the word for the fourth time, the young African man and woman begin to laugh but quickly stop when they see Ehmerney giving them a mean look.

"I don't have time for this... Sarah... Peter," Ehmerney then shouts. "Show these slaves where they will have to work!"

"Yes, Master!"

Once Ehmerney walks away, Sarah walks over to Karina. "If-he always this mean?" Karina asks Sarah

"Sometimes meaner, but don't let Master bother you, and no matter... You will always be Karina to me. Come now, let me show you where you and Lisa will be working."

Chapter 19

MOMENTS LATER, PETER AND SARAH ESCORT KARINA, Freddy, and Lisa to a field with thousands of cotton plants. As Karina stares, she sees hundreds of African men, women, and children picking cotton from the plants.

Peter then says, "Lisa, Freddy, and Karina, Master wants you to pick the cotton off these plants daily."

"We have to kneel down and pick the cotton off of these plants?" Lisa asks.

"That's right," Peter tells her.

"But that's too much work," Lisa complains. "And I'm tired."

"Lisa," Peter warns, "if you don't pick the cotton… you don't eat nor sleep."

"I don't eat? Well, in that case, hand me a bucket right now."

"Ar… are… we… required… to pick a certain amount of cotton?" Freddy stutters.

"Yes, Freddy," says Peter. "Everyone is required to pick their fair share of cotton."

"Peter," Karina asks, "what is every-one's fair share?"

"200 pounds per person," Peter tells her.

"200 pounds?" says Lisa.

"Yes," says Sarah. "And like Peter said, you don't eat nor sleep until you have picked your fair share."

"And whatever you do, don't let Jason see you not working. If so, he will tell Master, and you will get a good whipping," says Peter.

"Ja-son?" Karina then asks, "Who's Ja-son?"

"Oh, Jason is the overseer," says Sarah, "He's the one who watches us in the field and makes sure we are working and doing as we are told… Here he comes now!"

Karina sees a caramel-complexioned African man approaching on horseback. Sporting a bushy hair and beard, he rides with a very stern look on his face. Once in front of Karina and the others, he stops and jumps off his horse. Karina, who stands at five feet seven, sees Jason, who stands at only five feet two.

"Hello, Mr. Jason," says Sarah.

"Settle, Sarah," he responds with a big smile. "And who are these scraggly-looking bunch?"

"These are the new slaves: This is Lisa, Freddy, and Karina... I mean Denise."

For a second, Jason stands there and looks at them with his hands on his hips. "So... you are the new slaves, huh?" he then says as he sticks his lips out. "Well, I am Mr. Jason, the overseer of this here plantation, and Mr. Jason don't take no foolishness off of no one, especially no new slaves. So, do as you are told, or else I tell Master, and you'll get a good whipping. Do you hear me?"

"Yes, Jason," Karina and the others answer.

"I said it's Mr. Jason!" he demands as he stomps a foot.

"Yes, Mr. Jason," they answer.

"Okay then, so pick up a bucket and follow me."

After Karina, Lisa, and Freddy pick up their bucket, they begin following Jason. Walking hard through the cotton fields, he walks with his head up and chest out. "Hey, stop that hemp hampering and get back to work," he tells two African men who are talking.

"Yes, Mr. Jason," they answer as they quickly get back to work.

"Hey, Cindy," Jason then yells to an African woman who's walking the field while carrying a bucket filled with cotton. "I see you... I see you looking bootiful today." He then blows her a kiss. The African female pretends to catch Jason's kiss, and when Jason looks away, she throws his kiss off to the side.

"Okay, first stop," says Jason when he and the others come to a certain area of the field. "You... Freddy," he then says, "Get over here."

With a cautious look on his face, Freddy slowly walks toward Jason.

"What's the matter with you?" Jason says to him as he looks at him oddly. "You look like I'm gonna attack you or something."

"Na, na, no, Mr. Jay-son," stutters Freddy. "I, I, I, not afraid of you."

"Grrr," Jason suddenly screams as he playfully jumps at Freddy. Once Jason jumps toward him, Freddy drops his bucket, leans back, and covers his face. Jason, looking at his reaction, begins to laugh. "Oh my God, man, you are so fearful, imma starting calling you Fearful Freddy. Fearful

Freddy, get down here on the ground and start picking this here cotton off of these plants."

"Yes… Mr. Mr.…."

"Yeah, yeah, yeah, just starting picking." As Freddy begins picking, Jason says to Karina and Lisa, "Let's go to the next spot… follow me." They follow Jason a few feet, then stop. "This right here is your spot, Lisa, so come on and start picking!" Lisa slowly gets down to the ground. Once there, she picks one cotton ball off the plant… then stops.

"Why did you stop?" Jason answers

"I'm taking a break."

"Break? We don't take no breaks around here. No breaks until you pick your fair share of cotton, and you still got lots and lots of cotton to pick."

"But I'm tired!"

"You ain't tired girl, you just lazy… Lazy Lisa. That's who you are, you're Lazy Lisa. Now finish!"

"Fine," she growls as she resumes picking the cotton off the plants.

"Okay, now a place for you, Denise… follow me!"

Karina follows Jason to a nearby area. Once there, Jason says to her, "And here is your spot, Denise. Pick the cotton, and pick it well." Karina gets down on the ground and begins picking the cotton.

"Jason!" he suddenly hears a man call. Turing toward the direction from which he heard his name being called, Jason sees Ehmerney sitting on the front porch while smoking a cigar.

"Master!" Jason shouts with glee as he quickly runs toward him. There, he runs onto the porch. "Hello, Master," he excitedly says. "How are you doing today, Master? So nice to see you today, Master!"

"Jason, calm down," an annoyed Ehmerney tells him.

"I'm just so excited to be an overseer, Master. Thanks again for making me one."

"Well, be grateful to my father, because years ago, before his death, my father made a pact with the men in your family to use them as overseers. He made this pact with them because the men in your family were tall, strong, and they knew how to keep the slaves in order… then came you."

"What about me, Master?"

"Hum," he laughs as he looks him up and down. "Never mind. So how are the new slaves coming along?"

"Very well, Master. I trained them, and I trained them good, too. That Freddy is so fearful, so I calls him Fearful Freddy, and that Lisa she doesn't like to work, so I call her Lazy Lisa."

"And what about Denise?" Ehmerney asks as he watches her from the porch.

"I don't know about Denise quite yet, Master. She kind of quiet, so I haven't come up with a clever name for her yet, but I will."

Laughing, Ehmerney says, "I'm sure you will, Jason."

"Are you comfortable, Master?" Jason then asks. "Want a pillow for your back? Mrs. Ehmerney says how you have a bad back."

"I'm fine, Jason."

"Lemme get you a pillow for your back!" Jason scurries to a couch that's also on the porch and grabs a throw pillow. "Here, Master," he then says as he fluffs it. "Here's a pillow for your back!"

"Thank you, Jason." As Jason places the pillow behind Ehmerney's lower back, Ehmerney looks off to the side and rolls his eyes. Once leaning back on the pillow, he looks at Jason and quickly smiles, "Thanks, Jason."

"Oh, you welcome, Master. I do whatever I can to make you happy, Master."

"Yes, Jason, I know," Ehmerney says in a low tone.

"Oh, my goodness… Master!"

"What?"

"You have a big scuff mark on your boots. You want me to get it off for you? I can shine your boots. I can shine them really good, too."

"No Jason, you don't have to shine my boots… you're already licking them."

"Okay, Master."

Ehmerney then looks to the side to ponder a thought. "Jason?"

"Yes, Master!"

"Go get Denise and bring her here."

Upon Ehmerney's request, Jason quickly goes to the cotton field where Karina is stationed. "Denise!" he calls. However, she doesn't answer. "Denise," he calls once more and even louder; still Karina gives no reply. "Denise," he then screams. Jason then goes toward her and grabs her arm. Karina, caught off guard by his presence, looks at him wide-eyed. "Are you hard of hearing or something? Master wants you," he tells her as he points toward the porch.

Chapter 19

Karina sees Ehmerney sitting on the porch smoking a cigar. Standing to her feet, Karina walks toward the porch. "Yes, Mafter... I mean Mas...ter," she answers once she reaches the bottom of the stairs. For a moment, Ehmerney stares at her with a hard look. He then withdraws the cigar from his mouth and spits on both of his boots.

"I want you to polish my boots," he then tells her.

"Yes Mas...ter," Karina answers with a glazed look in her eyes. She then begins looking around.

"What are you looking for?" Ehmerney questions with an odd look on his face.

"A cloth, Mas...ter, so I can polish your boots."

Upon hearing Karina's response, Ehmerney leans forward and callously says, "Use... your... dress."

For a moment, Karina looks to the ground with tears in her eyes. She then slowly walks onto the porch, gets down on her knees, and begins polishing his boots.

"Yeah," says Jason as he watches with his hands on his hips. "And when you get finished, you can shine my boots too."

"Jason?"

"Yes, Master?"

"Go check on the field help and make sure they are doing as they are told."

"Yes, Master!"

Once Jason leaves, Ehmerney looks down at Karina shining his boots. "How come you didn't come when Jason first called you?"

"I forgot my name was Denise."

"Well, it *is* Denise," Ehmerney then shouts. "Your name is Denise. Denise, I tell you. Denise, and don't you forget it. You hear me?"

"Yes."

"Yes, what?"

"Yes, mas...ter."

"Well, my boots are shined now, so go back to the field... git"

"Yes Mas...ter."

Karina quickly gets up and begins leaving the porch. Halfway down the steps, Ehmerney calls, "Denise!"

"Yes Mas...ter," She turns and looks

"Just checking... Now git."

Karina turns and heads back to the field. Once there, she resumes picking cotton, and as she does, Ehmerney continues staring at her from the porch.

"My oh my," Martha suddenly says as she makes her way onto the porch. "It's so incredibly hot today," she adds as she sits on the couch. "Isn't it, Richard... isn't it, hot today?" Ehmerney, still focusing on Karina, gives no reply.

Martha then picks up a small silver bell and rings it, and within seconds a man with fair skin, short curly black hair, and green eyes comes onto the porch. As he arrives, he carries a silver tray that has a pitcher of lemonade and two empty glasses on top. Once the tray is placed on a small table beside the couch, the man picks up a glass, pours lemonade into it, and hands it to Martha. He then picks up another glass, pours lemonade into it, and says, "Sir," as he hands it to Ehmerney. Ehmerney, still staring at Karina, is unaware he's being handed the glass. 'Sir," the man says once more. However, Ehmerney's concentration remains unbroken.

Martha looks at Ehmerney and sees that he is staring at Karina. "Patrick," Martha then says to the man, "Give me the glass."

"Yes, Mrs. Ehmerney."

After the man hands the glass to Martha, she goes and stands within Ehmerney's view. Ehmerney suddenly looks at her.

"She's the one, isn't she?" says Martha. "She's the one you spent $2,000 on... It's her!"

"Yeah," Ehmerney lightly responds, "it's her."

"Oh, okay, so now it's *all* beginning to make sense. You didn't spend $2,000 on some field help; what you did was spend $2,000 so you could get yourself *another* mistress."

"What?... No!"

"Then why do you keep staring at her, Richard?"

Upon hearing the question, Ehmerney looks to the side but doesn't respond. Martha then hastily puts the glass down beside him and begins leaving the porch.

"Martha, wait!" Ehmerney shouts as he runs after her. "Wait!" he says once more as he stops her in the foyer of the house.

"Richard, are you cheating on me again?" an annoyed Martha asks with tears in her eyes. "Are you? Because my heart can't take this no more."

"No... no... it's not that way at all!"

"Then what is it, Richard? Tell me! Why do you keep staring at that girl?"

For a second, Ehmerney glances down at the floor. He then looks back at Martha and says, "Honestly... I guess I'm just trying to figure her out. There's something different about that girl."

"Like what?"

"I don't know. I can't seem to put my finger on it. All I know is that this girl... is not like any other slave we ever purchased before."

Martha then looks at Karina in the field from inside the house. Ehmerney, seeing Martha, stares at her as well.

Chapter 20

A S KARINA CONTINUES PICKING COTTON, SHE SEES PATrick on the porch putting a half-filled pitcher of lemonade and two glasses on a silver platter. Once the items are on the tray, he begins making his way inside, and as he does, he catches Karina's eyes. Patrick, now noticing Karina's stare, stops and stare in return. Karina then waves, "Hello." Not responding to her gesture, Patrick begins walking inside.

Moments later, a tired-looking Karina makes her way to a large cart that's nearly filled with picked cotton. Once in front of the wagon, she dumps the cotton she has in her bucket. She then turns and begins heading back toward the field, but stops when she notices a young, fair-skinned woman sweeping the back porch. "They have slaves that work inside the house?" Karina says as she stares oddly, "I wanna work inside the house." The woman, sensing Karina staring, stops sweeping and looks up. "Oh, hi there!" she says to Karina with a smile. "Haven't seen you here before, are you new?"

"I am."

"Well, welcome. My name is Isabell, and your name is?"

"Karina… I mean, Denise. No, Karina… honestly," she then laughs. "I don't know what my name is these days."

"Well… I like the name Karina, so I call you that. Are you hungry?"

"Very much so."

"Well, come to the steps." Karina goes and stands at the bottom of the stairs. "Now wait here," she tells Karina. She then turns and goes inside. Seconds later, Isabell returns with a slice of pie still in a round baking pan.

"Here," Isabell says, "Open your hands."

"Oh, but I can't," Karina says as she backs up a little. "I can't eat till I pick my fair share of cotton."

"Oh, don't worry... it will be our little secret. Come on, open your hands." Karina puts down the bucket and opens her hands, and Isabell puts the slice of pie into her hands.

"I made it this morning." After receiving the piece, Karina scarfs it down. "Oh my, I guess it was good, huh?" Isabell asks her.

"Very good!"

"Well, whenever you want a piece of pie, you be sure to stop past here... okay?"

"Okay. Tell me, Isabell, how long have you been here?"

"I've been on this plantation for about three years."

"And have you been working inside the house ever since?"

"I sure have!"

"Do they need help in the kitchen?"

"Boy, do they?"

"Well, maybe I can ask Master if I could work in the kitchen too. I love working in the kitchen. I used to help my mother in the kitchen all the time."

"That would be nice. Would love to have you."

"Okay, I'll ask Master when I see him. Well, I betta get back to work before Jason catches me."

"Yes, I reckon you, betta."

"Thanks again for the pie."

"You're welcome, Karina."

Karina begins heading back to the field. Once at the front of the house, she sees Ehmerney standing off the porch and watching the field with his hands on his hips. She begins walking toward him, when suddenly Jason approaches him. As she watches Jason eagerly talk to him, she says aloud, "Maybe I'll get a chance to talk to him later." Putting her head down, she sighs and heads back to the field.

Moments later, Karina dumps her filled cotton bucket into the carton once more, and after doing so, she sees Ehmerney standing alone near the back porch. Lightly inhaling then exhaling, she puts down her bucket and slowly walks over to him. "Hello Mas...ter," she nervously says with a smile.

Ehmerney looks at her oddly but doesn't say a word. Looking to the ground and clearing her throat, Karina says, "Mas...ter... I, I would like to make a special request."

"Special request?" He questions with a perturbed look on his face

"Yef, yef, Mas…ter. I would like to request to work in the kitchen. I'm good at kitchen work. I used to help my mother with kitchen work all the time."

"Is that so?"

"Yes, Mas-ter."

For a second, Ehmerney looks at her with an annoyed look on his face

"Come here!" he then aggressively says as he grabs her by the arm. He pulls her onto the back porch. Once there, he opens the back door to the kitchen and says, *"Look…look inside! …What do you see?"* Looking, Karina sees a host of men and women working in the kitchen… all who happen to be light-skinned. *"Do you see any dark-skinned slaves in here… do you?"*

"No," Karina lightly answers with tears now in her eyes

Slamming the door shut, he adds, *"So why on Earth do you think you're gonna work there? We don't have no dark-skinned slaves working inside the house, and you know why? 'Cause nobody wants to see no dark-skinned slaves in the house handling their food. That's why we keep them in the field."* Releasing her arm, he then says to her, *"Go back to the field where you belong, girl… git!"*

Running off the porch, Karina begins running toward the front of the house. "Get your bucket!" she suddenly hears Ehmerney scream. Turning back, she quickly grabs her bucket then resumes running back toward the front of the house. Once there, she stops then drops her bucket to the ground. Now trembling from head to toe, she covers her mouth as tears begin streaming down her face.

Chapter 21

THAT EVENING, AS KARINA SITS IN SARAH'S CABIN, SHE looks to the floor in deep though. "What's on your mind Karina," Sarah asks as she brushes her hair.

"Just thinking about Mas-ter. He was so mad at me today."

"Why? What did you do!?"

"I asked him if I-I could work in the kitchen."

"Huh?" Sarah gasps. "You asked Master if you could work in the kitchen?" she asks with wide eyes. "Oh, Karina. You still have yet to learn many things. They use the pretty ones for the house and the ones who look like you and me... we work the field."

As Sarah resumes brushing Karina's hair, Karina looks to the floor and ponders Sarah's words.

That night, as Karina lay on a wooden bed inside her own cabin, Sarah's words echo through her mind. She recalls hearing Sarah say, "They use the pretty ones for the house and the ones who look like you and me... we work the field."

Karina then begins to think back to a time she experienced in Africa. Thirteen-year-old Karina stands outside the orphanage. She sees a few feet ahead of her a fair-skinned teenage boy with dark hair and green eyes, and while kneeling, he constructs a wooden chair. Karina, leaning up against a wall, stares at him with starry eyes. Suddenly, another teenage boy approaches the one who's building the chair. He notices that Karina is staring at the boy who's building the chair, and he says to him, "Look!"

The boy building the chair glances up at Karina, then looks back down. "I think she likes you." The other boy tells him.

The boy building the chair responds, "Well, I don't like her... she's ugly."

As the flashback comes to an end, Karina places a hand over her heart as tears begin falling out of the corner of her eyes.

After a while, Karina drifts off the sleep, and as she sleeps, she dreams that she is standing on a wooden platform, with no clothes on, and in front of a crowd. Suddenly, an auctioneer stands beside her and says, "We have here today a female negro; she stands at five foot and a seven; she is young, heathy, and strong. She looks as though she would make a good house slave, but because she is so dark and ugly, you might want to keep her in the field."

"Dark and ugly," Karina suddenly hears someone say as they begin to laugh. "He called her dark and ugly." Looking off stage, Karina sees that the person who made the comment and who's now laughing is her brother Daniel. As Daniel continues to laugh, the people in the crowd begin laughing with him. At that moment, a ringing bell is heard from a distance.

Waking up! Karina hears a bell being rung. Sighing, she sits up and realizes it's morning. After sighing once more, she gets out of bed.

Moments later, as Jason rings a bell, slaves gather to receive their buckets. Karina, trailing behind, grabs a bucket and begins walking to the field. Now at the field, she begins picking cotton but stops and looks at all the dark-skinned people around her, and as she continues to stare, Sarah's words play back in her mind: "They use the pretty ones for the house and the ones who look like you and me... we work the field."

Hours later, Karina arrives at the wagon cart to dump the cotton she has collected all day. After doing so, she sees Isabell sweeping the back porch. For a moment, Karina stops and stare. She then begins walking away. "Oh, hi there, Karina," Isabell says when she sees Karina.

"Hi, Isabell," Karina coldly responds.

"Would you like a slice of apple pie? I just made it!"

"I have to go," Karina responds short as she hastily begins walking away. Once at the front, she stops for a second and looks to the ground in deep thought. Sighing, she picks her head up and goes back into the field.

Later that night in Sarah's cabin, as Karina sits in a chair, Sarah brushes her hair from behind. "Your hair is so long and thick, Karina," she hears Sarah say. "But it's dry... very dry. I go get some grease from a friend of mine to put in your hair... I be right back."

After Sarah has left the room, Karina looks and sees a small mirror in the room. Getting up from the chair, she goes toward the mirror. Now standing in front of the mirror, she stares aimlessly at herself, and as she does, the words Sarah spoke to her last night play back in her mind once more. She recalls hearing Sarah say, "They use the pretty ones for the house and the ones who look like you and me... we work the field."

She also recalls the auctioneer saying, "She looks as though she would make a good house slave, but because she is so dark and ugly, you might want to keep her in the field."

Her mind then drifts back to a time when she was sitting in her bedroom in Africa. As she sits on the edge of her bed, she says to Ruth while tears stream down her face, "He called me ugly, Mother. The boy called me ugly."

"God Almighty my child, come here," Ruth tells her as she extends her arms toward her. Once in Ruth's embrace, Ruth leads her to a mirror in the room. "Now Karina," says Ruth as they both look into the mirror, "tell me... what do you see when you look in the mirror?"

"What do you see?" Karina hears Ruth's voice echo throughout her mind. For a moment, Karina silently stares deeply into the mirror.

"I'm ugly," she then blurts out as tears begin to well up in her eyes. "I'm ugly... I'm so ugly... my skin is too dark, my lips... they're too big... even my eyes... they're too wide... I'm ugly... I'm ugly, I'm ugly, I'm ugly... dear God," she sobs. "I'm so ugly. I'm not fit to work in no house. I'm not fit to be anywhere. I'm ugly; I'm so ugly."

Just then, Sarah reenters the cabin. "Karina!" she then calls when she sees her standing at the mirror with tears running down her face. "What's the matter?"

With no response, Karina runs out of the cabin.

The next day, Karina walks to the wagon cart to dump her cotton, and when she does, she hears a female voice calling her name. "Karina!" She sees Isabell calling from the porch.

"Hello Isabell," Karina coldly responds.

"I made blueberry pie today... wanna slice?" For a moment, Karina stares at her with a look of resentment. She then turns and begins walking away, and as she does, Isabell calls, "Karina? Karina?"

Later that day, as the sun is going down, a gloomy-looking Karina sits alone on a log that's not too far from the back porch. She looks around and sees the other slaves enjoying an evening meal of cornbread and water. Suddenly, Freddy sits beside her, "Ha... ha... hello, Denise... Are you... okay? You... seem... sad."

"I'm fine, Freddy," she answers while still looking down.

For a moment, Freddy looks at her. He then reaches behind him and pulls up a small flower from the ground. "For you, De…nise," he says as he hands her the flower.

"Thank you, Freddy," says Karina as she gives a half smile.

At that moment, Lisa sits beside Freddy. "Hi, Freddy."

"Hi, Li-li-lisa"

"Hi, Denise."

"Hi, Lisa," Karina says gloomily.

"What's the matter?" Lisa then asks.

"Nothing," Karina lightly says.

"Here," Lisa then tells her. "Have a piece of my cornbread." Upon hearing her say that, Freddy looks at her wide-eyed. "What?" Lisa asks when she notices the expression.

"You don't never share your cornbread… e-ver."

"Oh, never mind you… here, Denise, here. Have a piece of my cornbread."

Slightly smiling, Karina takes a piece. "Thank you," she softly says.

With the tip of her fingers, Karina takes a piece of cornbread from Lisa's half and puts it into her mouth. Sarah sits beside her. "Hello, Karina, are you okay?" she asks as she wraps an arm around her. "I was worried about you last night when you ran out of the cabin crying… are you okay?"

"Oh my God, Freddy!" Lisa then shouts.

"What?"

"There's a spider crawling on your pants leg!"

Upon hearing Lisa's words, Freddy quickly jumps up and begins screaming a high-pitched sound as he violently tries to shake the spider off.

"Huh… I think it's gone, Freddy," Karina says with smirk.

"Are you sure?" he stops and asks as he looks himself over.

"Yeah, it's gone," says Lisa.

"It has to be gone. Probably even dead with all the shaking you just did," says Sarah.

"He looked so silly," says Karina as she begins to laugh.

"He did, didn't he?" says Sarah as she and Lisa begin laughing as well.

"Well, it was a really big spider," says Freddy.

However, his comment causes the women to laugh even louder. Freddy joins in on the laughter.

"You guys are such good friends to me," Karina then says as she places her arms around them.

Chapter 21

As Karina continues to laugh with her friends, Ehmerney watches from a distance while standing on the back porch. "Jason," he then calls as he sees him among the slaves.

"Yes, Master!" Jason answers with glee as he runs onto the porch.

"There's something I need you to do for me."

"What?"

Chapter 22

HOURS LATER IN SARAH'S CABIN, AS A DARK-SKINNED teenage boy named Tommy plays a flute that's made out of wood, Karina, Freddy, Sarah, and Peter folk dance to the music. Lisa, however, sits and watches. Once the music stops, they applaud, "That was fun," Karina says. "And Peter, your s-on Tommy playz that instrument very well."

"That's my boy," says Peter as he looks at him with pride in his eyes.

Just then, a knock is heard at the front door.

"Who on earth can it be at this hour?" asks Sarah. She opens the door to see Jason standing on the outside. "Yes?" she questions.

"I'm looking for Denise; is she here?"

"Well, ye—"

Before Sarah could finish her words, Jason impulsively comes inside. "Hey, Denise, Master wants you! He says you didn't pick your fair share of cotton. So, you gotta come back with me to the field."

"Now?" Peter questions. "But it's dark out."

"So," Jason responds. "What Master says… goes. So, come on, Denise… come on."

With a perplexed look on her face, Karina slowly makes her way toward the door while looking at the others.

"It's okay, Karina. It's okay," Sarah tells her. "We'll be here when you get back."

Chapter 23

MOMENTS LATER, AS JASON MAKES HIS WAY TO THE cotton field, Karina trails behind, and as she does, she fearfully looks at the tall evergreen trees that are blowing carelessly in the wind.

"Here you go," she suddenly hears Jason say as he hands her a bucket.

"But I picked my fair share today... I know I did." Karina tells him.

"Well, Master said you didn't, so start the picking." With a fearful look in her eyes, Karina goes into the field, gets down on her knees, and begins picking, and as she does, she looks and sees Ehmerney. Sitting in a rocking chair, he watches from the porch while smoking his cigar.

"Hoot, hoot, hoot," Karina suddenly hears. Startled by the sound, she looks and sees an owl perched on a nearby tree branch. Looking back at the porch, she sees that Ehmerney is no longer sitting there. Sighing, she resumes picking cotton. A sudden sound of thunder coming from the sky causes her to jump.

"Oh... no," she then says as she looks up. "Please don't let it rain... please." However, rain begins to fall. "Oh," shouts Karina as she runs from the field and onto the porch. Once there, she stares as rain begins to fall heavily.

"What are you doing on the porch?" Ehmerney shouts as he comes from inside the house.

"It's... it's... rain-ing!"

"I don't care what it's doing. Get off the porch... Git!" Karina runs off the porch but stops just beyond the stairs. "And you finish picking that cotton, you hear?" Ehmerney demands, and in the pouring rain, Karina kneels to the ground and continues picking cotton. She tries her best to see what she is doing, but the constant water falling in her face makes it difficult to do so.

Moments later, in the still-pouring rain, Karina carries a bucket filled with white, soggy cotton. She makes her way to the barn where the wagon cart that's filled with dry cotton has been stationed. Nearly a few feet away from the door, she trips and falls face-first into a muddy puddle. Slowly standing up, she looks and realizes she's now completely covered in mud. She begins wiping herself off when suddenly, she hears a man wickedly laughing. Looking toward the sound, she sees Ehmerney standing on the back porch while laughing hysterically. As he continues to laugh, he turns and goes inside the house. Karina, now standing alone in the pouring rain, picks up her bucket. She begins heading toward the barn but stops.

"Ahhhhh," Karina screams as she chucks the bucket across the muddy ground. She then turns and leaves the field.

In Sarah's cabin, Sarah, Lisa, and Freddy sit by a burning fireplace. Suddenly, the front door to the cabin ferociously flies open, causing a dish that's sitting on the shelf to fall to the floor and break. Sarah, Lisa, and Freddy wonder what on Earth could have caused such a commotion, and what they see is Karina standing outside the door with an angry look on her face.

As they continue to stare, the sound of thundering is heard coming from up above as the flickering light from the lighten is seen on her face. Karina then slowly stomps inside the cabin while Sarah, Lisa, and Freddy warily stand to their feet. Once inside, Karina stops just beyond the door-way, then slams the door behind her. Freddy quickly stands behind Lisa. "Karina," Sarah then softly asks, "are you okay?" Karina, still standing in place, looks straight ahead but doesn't utter a single word. "Karina," Sarah asks again as she slowly approaches her, "are you okay?"

"He laughed," she then says as she continues staring forward.

"What?" Sarah questions.

"He laughed," Karina repeats.

"Who, Karina… who laughed?"

"Mas-ter. I was going to the barn to put my picked cotton into the wagon, and while doing so, I tripped and fell into a muddy puddle, and when I did… he laughed."

"Oh Karina," Sarah then says, "Don't let Master…"

"He laughed!" Karina angrily interrupts

Just then, a knock is heard at the front door. Sarah opens the door to Jason, aggressively sticking his head inside. "Is Denise in here?" he asks. Seeing her standing there, he forces his way inside. "Hey, Denise," he then says as he walks toward her. "What do you think you're doing?" he asks her as he grabs her by the arm and faces her toward him. "You get back outside and finish picking that cotton."

"No!" Karina screams as she pushes him away. The intensity of her push causes Jason to fly backward, forcibly hitting the doorway.

"Okay, you know what, Denise?" he then tells her. "Finish it tomorrow." He then turns and quickly leaves the cabin.

Once Jason has left, Karina angrily looks at everyone in the cabin. She then goes toward the front door, harshly opens it, and walks into the still-pouring rain, and as she disappears into the night, thunder is heard coming from the sky.

Chapter 24

OMENTS LATER, THE RAIN HAS STOPPED, BUT A STILL-wet Karina sits in the woods. As she sits, she stares aimlessly at the mountains that appear through a forest opening, and she stares with fingers over her mouth. Suddenly, she hears soft footsteps approaching from behind. Turning towards the sound, she sees Abaven standing there.

"You!" she says, wide-eyed.

"Me!" he responds with a slight smile.

Karina then turns and resumes staring at the mountains, and while doing so, Abaven sits beside her. While staring, Karina begins to say, "My fa-ther once t-old me… that e-very person haz a breaking point… e-very person haz a *limit* to how much they can take. Well… tonight… I found that limit… When I was captured and caged like a wild animal… I thought I was going to break… But I didn't. When I was put into that horrible, horri-ble dun-geon and *forced* to stand in God knowz what… I knew for s-ure that I was going to break… But I did not. And when I was strapped to the floor of that ship where other African people were packed tightly beside me, above me and even beneath me… I *maintained* my composure. And *what* iz my reward for enduring s-uch hard-ships…what iz my reward? My reward iz that now I have the *dis-tinct plea-sure* of working as a sl-ave on a planta-tion for the rest of my life!…

"A place… where I am forced to pick cotton until my handz bleed. A place… where I am forced to wipe the spi-ttle off a man's bo-ots even if that man laughs at me. A place… where I am treated like I'm some kind of hid-eous creature all because my sk-in is *too dark*. A place where I am laughed at, talked down to, and treated like cattle… Hum… Hell… even the cattle gets treated better. And if for some *odd* reason that I or any other African, for that matter, is not fit to be *used*… then we are cazt a-side as if we are *nothing*. Just like that woman who was thrown off the s-hip and fed to the shar-ks. She was cazt aside like an old dirty rag. And you know what'z really sad, Abaven; do you wanna know what'z really so sad... is that I actually envied that woman... I did... I still do... I envy her. She might have died a mi-ser-able death... but at least she'z not like me, who's st-ill here... *suf-fering.*"

"Karina," softly then says Abaven, "I know that you are hurting right now but—"

"But what, Abaven?" Karina interjects. "What? What are you going to tell me... that God is *with* me? Is that what you're going to tell me, Abaven, huh? Is that what you're going to tell me? That God is *with* me? Well, tell me, Abaven... tell me... was God with that woman on the s-hip when she got c-ast overboard? Or how about the many upon many of Afri-cans who never made it this far because they died during the voyage over here... was God with them, too? You come here tonight trying to comfort me... but no Abaven... No! You don't bring me no comfort tonight. Tonight! ...You gonna feel my pain. Tonight...*you* are going to know *exactly* what it fe-els like... *to be me!*

"To live a *life* where it fe-els as tho you can't even breathe. A life... where it fe-els as if your own self-happi-ness, self-love, self-worthi-ness is all on borrowed time. A life where you can't even... dream freely, believe freely, hope freely... *obtain* freely, and if you dare to do so... if you dare... then you are punished. A life where the *world* makes you feel as tho you are a flower being *pressed* into the sand... until it becomes no more. You say that God is here, Abaven? You say that God is a God of sun-shine... and that God is a God of rain... but what you *failed* to mention, Abaven, is that God... is also a *mean* God, a *cruel* God. A God who does not care about the suf-fering of people.

"A God," she says as tears begin to well up in her eyes, "who I don't think loves me very much." As tears begin to cascade down her face, she adds, "I don't think God loves *us* very much... I don't think... he loves us at all." Upon saying such words, Karina covers her face and begins to sob heavily.

"Oh, Karina," says Abaven as he reaches out to console her.

"No," Karina then shouts as she jumps up and quickly moves away. "Don't touch me, Abaven! Don't touch me, don't touch me, don't touch me, don't touch me, don't touch me, don't touch me, don't touch me... don't... don't..." Turning away, Karina lets out a big gasp. She then stretches out her arms, falls to her knees, and wails.

Chapter 24

Slowly approaching her, Abaven kneels beside her. He begins wrapping his arms around her, but Karina suddenly shouts, "No!" Jumping up, she runs away. She attempts to run through the forest but is unable to do so due to the tears that blur her vision. She is then met with a large pine tree that stops her in her tracks, and there at the tree, she positions her back against the bark, then slides down until her legs are flat on the ground.

As she sits there and cries, her mind begins flashing back to various moments of her past. Karina recalls seeing her mother (Ozigbodi) standing before her, smiling with her arms stretched out wide. She recalls the moment when she saw her mother being dragged away while being trapped in a net. She remembers being in her father's (Donkor) arms as he spun her around while they hugged face to face. She remembers her thirteen brothers hugging and playing with her. She remembers the time when she sat at the table with Ruth, Kevin, and her five brothers while eating breakfast, and she recalls the moment when she sat in the boat and watched as Africa disappeared in the fog.

Her grief causes her to lie completely on the ground. She looks up and sees stars in the sky, and as she stares, she remembers watching the stars with her father. Suddenly, dark clouds begin to cover them. "Don't go," she sobs as she watches the concealment. "Please... don't leave me... please." However, the stars become hidden. "Oh God," she then cries while still lying on the damp, hard ground. After crying to the point of exhaustion, Karina drifts off to sleep, and as she sleeps, she dreams.

Chapter 25

KARINA DREAMS THAT SHE'S STANDING ON THE DECK OF A ship. AS she looks around in astonishment, she sees a cloudy sky where seagulls fly. "No!" She suddenly hears a woman scream. Looking, Karina sees two soldiers forcibly taking an African woman to the edge of the deck.

"No!" Karina shouts as she quickly runs towards the scene. Once there, she sees the woman being cast overboard. "No," Karina screams as she watches the woman descend to the waters where numerous sharks wait below. However, just before the woman hits the water, Karina looks away. Placing her back against the ship's rail, Karina squats down. "Oh my," she says as she covers her mouth while trembling. "My God... my God, my God, my God. I don't think God loves us very much," Karina then says as she begins to sob. "I don't think he loves us at all." She then buries her face into her knees and cries heavily. Suddenly, the wind begins to blow. Lifting her face from her knees, she looks around to see what might be the reason for such a change. Slowly standing to her feet, she looks out toward the ocean. Her mouth and eyes open wide when she sees...

...thousands of African people in white robes ascending from the waters, and as they ascend, they head toward the sky that welcomes them with open clouds and beams of light. She then sees the African woman who was recently cast overboard rising from the ocean. Dressed in a white robe as well, she stops, looks at Karina, smiles, then continues soaring upward.

"God Almighty," Karina then says as she watches in awe, "It's beau-ti-ful... Just beau-ti-ful. I s-ure do wish I could go," she says as she looks down at the ocean. "I wanna go," she says as she looks back toward the sky. "I'm going!... Wait!" Karina then shouts. "Wait for me...I'm coming," she says as she begins climbing over the ship's rail. "I'm coming. I'm com-ing... wait!" Now standing outside the ship's ledge, she looks down and sees a host of sharks waiting for her to jump. "God Almighty... It's a lot going on down there, but better that than bon-dage." She then closes her eyes, takes a deep breath, and prepares to jump. However, before doing so, a soldier pulls her back inside the boat.

"No!" Karina screams, "Let me go... I wanna go. I wanna go. I don't wanna be here. Let me go, so I can go to heaven!" Nonetheless, the soldier pulls her from the edge and then chains her to a pole. "No," Karina cries, "No... I wanna go," she sobs. "I wanna go to heaven." As she continues to cry, she watches as the last person ascends into heaven. Then the beams of light disappear, and the clouds grow dark.

"No," Karina cries, "Don't leave me here." Suddenly, a ringing bell is heard from a distance. Waking up, she realizes that she had fallen asleep on the ground underneath the large pine tree. The ringing bell that was heard in her sleep is actually the calling bell for the slaves to report to the field. As she continues to lie there, she sees a number of slaves walking toward the field.

Moments later, a gloomy-looking Karina arrives to receive her bucket, and after doing so, she looks and sees Sarah, Lisa, and Freddy looking at her with paranoid expressions. For a slight moment, Karina stops and stare in return. She then proceeds walking forward, but she stops when a comment her mother Ruth once made suddenly comes to mind.

Karina remembers a time when she was sitting in the living room of the cabin in Africa. As she angrily sits there, she remembers hearing Ruth say, "I know you are angry right now, I know you are, but you can't hurt the ones you love or even the ones who love you."

As the flashback comes to an end, Karina turns and goes back towards Sarah, Lisa, and Freddy. There, she puts her bucket down and gives them a hug. "I'm sorry." She then looks at Sarah and says, "Oh dear. Look at your hair," she tells her as she rubs it. "Better come to my cabin this evening so I can fix it."

"Yeah?" Karina questions.

"Yes," says Sarah.

As Karina renders a smile, she and Sarah give each other a hug. Karina then picks up her bucket and resumes heading toward the field.

Hours later, a still-glum Karina picks cotton in the field but stops when her eyes lay hold of Ehmerney coming out of the house. As she watches him make his way to the barn, she visualizes standing over top of him and violently hitting him with her bucket. Ehmerney, on the ground, screams as he tries his best to shield his bloody face with his bloody hands.

Letting out a loud sigh, Karina resumes picking cotton, and she continues picking when suddenly an image grabs her attention. Looking into the distance, Karina sees a man standing on a hill. He's wearing a thin white jacket that reaches to his knees, and underneath his jacket, he sports a royal blue button shirt, black pants, and shoes; around his neck is a gold tie.

"Stop daydreaming!" Karina suddenly hears Jason say as he steps into her view. Upon hearing his words, Karina quickly begins picking. Once Jason has walked away, she discreetly glances back at the spot where she once saw the man standing but sees him nowhere in sight.

Later in the day, Karina goes toward the wagon cart to dump her picked cotton. However, just before doing so, she sees the man again, this time standing underneath a tree that's only a few feet away. "Come on, hurry up and dump your bucket!" Karina hears a woman behind her say.

"Oh... sorry," Karina replies as she quickly dumps her bucket then moves out of the way. Looking back at the spot where she saw the man standing, Karina sees that he's no longer there.

That evening, as the sun begins to set, Karina sits on a log alone and watches as everyone eats and socializes. Standing to her feet, she begins walking away when suddenly she sees the man standing beside the barn. Stopping in place, she stares at the man, who motions for her to come closer. He then turns and walks behind the barn. Slowly and cautiously, Karina follows him. Once behind the barn, she sees the man standing there while looking at the mountains. As she slowly approaches him, she sees a silver object around his neck. One end made out of metal is shaped like a large heart, while the other end has a round metal piece that's attached to a black tube. "Hello Karina," the man says, looking at her.

For a moment, Karina stares without saying a word. "Are you an angel?" she then softly asks.

"More so a descendant."

"A de-scen-dant? Who's de-scen-dant?"

"Yours... eight generations removed."

"But that's im-pos-sible."

"With God... all things are possible, Karina."

"Hum, God... so I guess he sent you here to tell me something, right?"

"He did."

"What? To remind me that he's with me and that he lo-ves me?"

"I come with a different message, a message you probably never heard before, but a message that's worth hearing."

"The only message I want to hear is the message of death. I want for God to take me out of here."

"I understand."

"Do you now? You understand how I feel with your clean white jacket and your sh, sh, shiny shoes. Look at my handz... look at them! They're bruised and bloody from picking cotton all day, and I don't know which is worse, how I feel on the outside or how I feel on the inside. I feel like I am nothing. I don't even feel like a true African anymore. My parents and my brothers fought to the death, but not me—oh, no, I was too frightened. Now I am here in this God for, for, for-saken place."

"Your feelings are true, and part of what you are experiencing is survivor's remorse."

"What?"

"Survivor's remorse... It's a term used in the future. It's when people around you die but you survive, and because of that, you feel guilty."

"I do feel guilty... some-times I don't know if God allowed for others to die because he was punishing them or if he kept me here because he was punishing me."

"Neither. God loved those who have perished, and he accepted them into his kingdom, but he left you here on Earth because he still has a purpose for you here."

"Really... purpose... me? I don't think so."

"Karina, let me show you something... Look; look toward the mountains!"

Looking, Karina sees thousands of people coming down from the mountain. People of all ages, races, and genders. Once they reach the bottom, they stop and happily stare at Karina.

"Who are all those people?" Karina asks as she stares in awe

"Those people... are all your descendants."

"All of them?"

"All of them, and they are all waiting on you, Karina. They are all counting on you to be strong. I know you are hurting right now. I know you are, and I know you want to give up, and I don't blame you. I can't even begin to imagine what you must be going through, but you can't give up, Karina; you can't. If so, then all those people that you see will never come to be... I... will never come to be.

"Karina, if you choose to continue, one day someone will tell me your life's story, and it will be your story that will inspire me to become a doctor.

You see… they need you, Karina… I need you. Please, Karina, please! Make a choice to be strong… for us. Please, Karina, or should I say… Mama Karina." Upon hearing the man's words, Karina takes another look at the people and then back at the man.

That night, as Karina sits in the woods, she stares aimlessly at the mountains that appear through a forest opening. "They are all waiting on you, Karina," she remembers hearing the man say. "They are all counting on you to be strong."

"Dear God Almighty," Karina then says aloud. "Throughout the course of my lifetime, I have found myself surrounded by many troubled waters… troubled waters that nearly forced me to surrender. Yet in the midst of my pain and sorrow, I have gained an awakening. I have come to realize that there is something far greater than who I am, how I feel, or what I am even going through. Now, I realize… that somebody, somewhere is counting on me to be strong… so with this new thought in mind… I shall stay strong. I should… I can… I will… Done! Because now I know that my life truly serves a purpose… purpose… me."

After saying these words, Karina looks to her left and sees the man in the white jacket leaning up against a tree. Standing up, she goes toward him, and as she draws close to him, he draws close to her. Now standing before each other, Karina lovingly caresses the side of his face. Once her hand reaches his lips, he kisses it. The man then goes and stands in front of another tree, and while standing there, he looks at Karina and smiles. His image then transforms into a multitude of stars that fly into the sky. As the stars reach the cloudy sky, the clouds move away, allowing the stars to fill the night sky.

As Karina looks toward the now starry sky, she can't help but smile. Looking away, nearby cabins capture her view. She then goes toward the forest opening and stares at the plantation. "Purpose me," she then says while staring. "Purpose… me," and with her head up and a smile still on her face, she makes her way toward her cabin.

Chapter 26

THREE YEARS LATER, ON A CLOUDY MORNING OF SEP-
tember 11, 1811, a now nineteen-year-old Karina sits alone in a
cabin. As she sits there with her eyes closed, she recites a saying that
was once taught to her by her mother, Ruth.

"I am a child of God. I am fearfully and wonderfully made. I am attractive, intelligent, and str-, str... come on, Karina." She opens her eyes
and says to herself, "Str-ong," she slowly pronounces. "I'm attractive, intelligent, and... *strong*, and I do have the power to show s-elf-control... This
is my mind-set! I said it, Mother!" she happily says as she jumps to her feet
and looks toward the ceiling. "I said the words that we often said before
bible study!" Her smile then slowly dissipates as she looks towards the
floor. "Oh Mother," she then says, "How I miss you and Father so. I pray
that I shall see you both again someday."

Just then, a ringing bell is heard, followed by a knock at the cabin door.
Karina opens the door to see Lisa, Freddy, and Sarah standing at the entrance. "Well, another day has come," says Sarah. "Figured we could all
walk together."

"I would love that!" says Karina

As the four of them begin heading toward the field, Freddy calls, "Karina!"

"Yes, Freddy."

"As we were coming to your cabin, we heard you saying something
about being a child of God... what was that about?"

"Oh, I was just saying something my mother taught me to say ever
since I was little."

"Can you say it again?" asks Sarah. "We would love to hear it."

"Okay," says Karina, "It goes like this: I am a child of God. I am fearfully and wonderfully made. I am attractive, intelligent, and *str...ong*, and
I do have the power to show s-elf-control. This is my mindfet... set, I
mean."

"Wow, those are some powerful words, Karina," says Lisa.

"They sure are," says Freddy.

"Well, I'm glad you think so," Karina tells them.

As the four of them continue to walk, a heavyset, dark-skinned African woman watches from a few feet away. "Oh, my goodness, those *are* some powerful words," she says out loud. "Wait till I tell Daddy what I just heard." She then turns and quickly walks away.

Moments later, Karina, Sarah, Freddy, and Lisa approach a ringing bell that's being rung by Jason. "Well, look who finally decided to show up," says Jason. "Settled Sarah, Fearful Freddy, Lazy Lisa, and… and…" He stops when he gets to Karina. "Denise," he then says. "Dang gone it, I still haven't come up with a clever name for you yet, Denise… but I'm sure I will."

"I'm sure you will too, Jason," Karina responds with a smirk.

Once the four of them get their buckets, they begin heading toward the field, and as they do, they hear Jason shout, "And remember, no breaks or eating till you pick your fair share."

Upon hearing Jason's words, Karina stops in place. "What, Karina?" Sarah then asks as she and the others look at her oddly.

"I have an idea," Karina tells them.

"What?" Lisa asks.

Karina then whispers to the three of them.

"Okay," says Lisa with a light laugh as Sarah and Freddy nod their heads yes. "Let's do it."

The four of them then turn, look at Jason, and say with a big, cheesy smile, "Yes, Mr. Jason!"

"That's right," says Jason happily as he places his hands on his hips and looks to the sky. His smile then dissipates when he looks to the ground to ponder their actions.

As Karina, Sarah, Freddy, and Lisa approach the field, Ehmerney watches from the porch. "Master," Isabell says as she walks up beside him. "I made some oatmeal raisin cookies for Mrs. Ehmerney's tea party today. Would you like to try one?" Upon hearing her query, Ehmerney looks at her, then down at the cookies, and as he stares, his mind flashes back to an earlier time on the plantation. Just seventeen years of age, he comes out of the house while carrying a cloth-covered basket filled with oatmeal raisin cookies. Stepping off the porch, he sees nearby an African male slave chopping wood. With a smile on his face, he heads toward him. "Hello!" he says once standing there.

"Hi," the slave gloomily responds.

"How are you doing today?" Ehmerney then asks.

The slave responds with a bizarre look.

"I guess that was a dumb question." Ehmerney then looks to the side and lowly says once realizing he asked an unnecessary question. "Well... my mother made some oatmeal raisin cookies today... would you like to try one?" he then says with a smile as he extends the basket towards the slave.

"Master," he then hears Isabell say as the flashback ends, "would you like to try one?"

"No," he hastily responds. "I don't want any cookies."

"Yes, Master." Isabell then turns and goes back inside the house. Ehmerney resumes watching Karina in the field. Letting out a big sigh, he then leaves the porch and goes inside.

In the barn sits a very old African man, placing picked cotton into burlap bags, and as he continues, the heavyset, dark-skinned African woman enters.

"Daddy," she loudly says, "I got something to tell you!"

"What is it, Virginia?" the old man replies with a raspy voice.

"Daddy, God done answered our prayers. You know how we been praying for God to send us someone new to speak to the slaves at the fire circle since you can't speak no more. Remember, Daddy, huh... remember?"

"Yes, Virginia, I remember."

"Well, God done answered our prayers. He sent someone new to speak to the slaves at the fire circle."

"He has!"

"Yup, he sure has!"

"Well, who might this person be?"

With a big smile, Virginia says...

Chapter 27

"KARINA!" SHE HEARS SOMEONE CALL HER NAME AS SHE DUMPS A FILLED bucket of picked cotton into the wagon cart. Turning towards the voice, she sees Virginia walking toward her. "Girl," Virginia says once beside her, "I heard what you said this morning."

"What did I zay... I mean... s-ay?"

"About being a child of God,"

"Oh yeah, that," she replies with a light laugh, "Well, it was something my mother taught me to s-ay."

"Well, it was bootiful, girl. Just plain bootiful."

"I'm sorry, but who are you, and how do you know my name?"

"I'm Virginia, and I know a lot of what goes on around here. I even know where you stay."

"Well, that's comforting," Karina says off to the side with a paranoid look on her face.

"Listen, every night, me and some of the slaves gather around a fire in the woods to sing songs, then someone shares a special word. Wanna come?"

"Well, where is it?"

"Child, please, you don't need to worry about that. I will show you the way. I just come by your place tonight and get you. So, you coming?"

"Ye-s, I'll come."

"Good. Well, lemme get outta here before Jason catches us chit-chatting, and you know what a snitch he can be. See ya later, Karina."

"Bye... Virginia?... God Almighty," Karina then says as she looks to the ground. "Why do I feel like I just got hit by a human hurricane?" For a second, Karina glances at Virginia walking away. She then looks back toward the ground, and while staring, she shakes her head, laughs, and then walks away.

That evening, while Karina sits alone in the cabin, a knock is heard at her front door. Opening the door, she sees Abaven standing on the other side. "May I come in?" he asks.

"Of course." As Abaven makes his way inside, Karina says to him, "Ho-nest-ly Abaven, I don't understand why you bothered to knock. You could have just appeared here."

"Well, I could have, but I prefer to get your permission first. When I asked if I could come in, I wasn't just talking about coming into your cabin, but also into your heart."

"I just think it's ama-zing how you st-ill vi-sit me."

"You sound surprised."

"I am."

"But why?"

"Because of that one night when you came to visit me, that night when I was so angry... I screamed at you Abaven... and it was-n't even your fault."

"Karina, it's okay," Abaven says as he stands in front of her and grabs both hands. "I'm not offended. Really. I'm not. I understand because I realize that anger is just a normal human emotion. Anger is actually passion turned inward. If you didn't care so much about your life as well as the lives of others, then you wouldn't have gotten so angry. So, if you ever have a moment in your life when you want to be angry... then go ahead... be angry. If you want to be sad... then be sad. Even if you want to be happy, then be happy. But whatever you decide to be... know this... I will always be here for you. I will listen to you when you scream, I will be that shoulder to cry on when you are sad, and I will even dance with you when you are happy. Whatever you do, I will always be here for you, Karina... always."

"You will?" Karina says with tears in her eyes.

"Yes, Karina, I will," Abaven happily responds.

Karina and Abaven then give each other a hug.

"But now I have to get ready to go," he abruptly tells her as he withdraws from the embrace.

"Abaven?" Confused, Karina calls out when she sees him heading toward the door.

"Well, I'm sorry, but my father needs me on another assignment... but I'll be back though... I promise... Oh, and by the way," he says just before exiting. "I don't care what anyone says... dark-skinned people... are absolutely beautiful." And with a wink, he leaves the cabin.

Chapter 27

Now standing in the cabin alone, Karina blushes as she covers her mouth with her hands. As she turns away from the door, she hears someone enter.

"Oh, Abaven," she happily says as she turns back around. "You're, bac—" but her statement is cut short when she sees Virginia standing there.

"You ready?" she then asks

"I guess," Karina oddly replies. "Although it would have been nice for you to knock first," she adds in a low voice.

"What?" Virginia asks

"Nothing," says Karina, "I'm ready."

"Alright then, come on." As Karina trails behind her, the shining of the moon allows her to see a black branded mark on the upper left corner of Virginia's back.

"God Almighty," Karina then says as she begins looking at the tall pine trees. "Thes-e pine tre-es s-ure do look s-cary at night." A sudden breeze causes the trees to move like creatures in the night.

"Wait!" she then exclaims as she begins running towards Virginia. "Wait for me! Where are we going anyhow?" Karina asks once beside her.

"Hold your horses, child. You'll see."

Suddenly, the flickering of a yellow and orange light is seen up ahead. "Is that it? Is that the fire circle?" Karina asks, but Virginia gives no reply. As Karina continues to stare, her perception is confirmed as she witnesses the growing intensity of the heat accommodated by the sparks flying in the crisp night air.

As she watches the tiny spurs of flame fly past her, she says to herself, "Why does all of thif feel s-o familiar?"

Now only a few feet away, the silhouettes of people sitting around the fire come into view. Once at the circle, Karina realizes that the people sitting around the fire... are actually African people of various ages and genders, and as they sit there, they softly sing while staring intensely at the fire.

"Well, here we are, Karina," Virginia tells her. "Have a seat, and I will introduce you."

Looking to her left, Karina sees a woman making room for her on the log. "Here... have a seat," the woman then tells her, as she pats the now empty spot beside her.

"Thank you," says Karina as she takes a seat beside her.

Once seated, Karina looks across the circle and sees an old African man staring at her with a smile, and as he continues to do so, he nods.

"Hello, Daddy," Virginia then says to the old man as she stands in the middle of the circle. "And hello, everyone," she then loudly says to the crowd. As Virginia begins to speak, their singing comes to an end. "I brought a very special person to the fire circle tonight. A very special young lady whose name is Karina. Karina has spoken some very special words earlier today, words that were deep, real deep. Now some of you might look at her and say, 'But this girl is young,' and indeed, she is young. However, when you listen to what this young girl has to say, you will come to realize the depth of wisdom she has flowing through her veins.

"So, I present to you at this time... Ms. Karina, and as she comes, I ask that you open up your hearts, your minds, and your spirits to receive her special words. Ms. Karina." Virginia then looks at her and says, "Share with *us* your special words."

After receiving such an introduction, Karina stands to her feet. "Hello, everyone," she says as she looks around the circle. "Thanks s-o much for having me here tonight." She then looks to the ground to ponder her next words. Looking back up, she adds, "And I'm really glad to be here." Karina then sits back down.

After Karina has seated, Virginia looks at her Dad, who's staring at her with an odd expression.

"Uh, Karina," Virginia then asks, "don't you have some *more* special words you would like to share?"

"Nope." She looks at Virginia and says, "That's it."

Karina, now noticing the look of confusion on Virginia's face, says to her, "What?"

Chapter 28

MOMENTS LATER, AS KARINA LEAVES THE FIRE CIRCLE with Virginia, Karina says to her, "Virginia, I'm sorry, but I didn't know that you invited me to the fire circle to peak, I mean... s-peak, or else I would not have come. I don't speak to no crowds of people."

"And why not?" Virginia stops and asks.

"I'm shy, and I can't even zay, I mean s-ay words correctly... See what I mean?"

"Karina, I don't know what you see, but I see a person who God has called to speak. Never mind you being shy or not saying words correctly; never mind all of that. God has called you to speak, girl."

"No." Karina shakes her head while backing away slowly. "No," she says with the word barely ghosting between her lips. "No," she says louder. "No!" she then screams as she runs toward her cabin. "I'm not spea-king to no crowds of people, Virginia... no!"

Now inside, she closes the door, then pins her back toward it, and as she stands there, she remembers a moment she once experienced with her mother, Ruth, while in her bedroom at the cabin in Africa. She remembers asking Ruth, "What plan does God have for me?"

Ruth replies, "I truly believe God will use you to speak words of comfort to others."

"No," Karina then says as the thought comes to an end. "I'm not peak-ing to no crowds of people... No!" She then jumps into bed and pulls the cover up over her head.

The next day, while Karina picks cotton in the field, Ruth's words echo in her mind: "I truly believe God will use you to speak words of comfort to others."

Her thought is then interrupted when she suddenly hears a woman screaming and even crying. Looking up, Karina sees an African woman running behind a wagon, and in the back of the wagon sits a twelve-year-old African boy. As he reaches out toward the woman, he cries profusely while screaming, "Mama, Mama!" The woman reaching out to her son tries her hardest to catch up to the wagon but is unable to do so as the wagon rides even faster.

Once the wagon has ridden off property, the woman falls to her knees and with her arms stretched out wide, she says, "They took him... They took my boy. Oh God, oh God, oh God... why?" Exhaling deeply, she then screams, "Why!" She then pins her face to the ground and cries uncontrollably. Karina, still looking, feels tears welling up in her own eyes.

Later in the day, as Karina dumps a bucket of picked cotton into the wagon cart, she hears the bell being rung. "A ringing bell in the middle of the day," she says to herself. "What on Earth for?"

Going toward the bell, she sees Peter's son Tommy nearby, strapped to a wooden post with his bare back exposed. "Gather around, everyone," Jason then says. "Master has something to tell y'all."

Karina then sees Ehmerney walking toward Tommy, and while doing so, he holds a book in one hand and in the other... a whip. Now standing beside Tommy, Ehmerney says to everyone, "This young slave niwas caught reading. Reading for slaves is forbidden on this plantation, and if you didn't know that before, you will know it today. Today, you will see what happens to a slave if they are ever caught reading or even writing on this plantation." Standing back from the wooden post, Ehmerney begins whipping Tommy, and with every lash felt, he cries out in agony.

"God Almighty," Karina gasps as she looks on with tears in her eyes.

Karina then sees Peter standing nearby. Looking at him, she notices that he has tears streaming down his own face, and with every lash given, his body shakes as if he's the one receiving the beating. "Peter," Karina then goes over to him and says, "Isn't that your son Tommy?"

"It is," he sadly answers.

"Oh Peter, I'm *so* sorry."

"So am I. I told that boy so many times to stop that reading... Master don't like it when slaves read. He thinks it gives them ideas."

Upon hearing Peter's words, Karina sorrowfully continues watching Peter's son getting whipped.

Later that evening, Ehmerney rides horseback onto the property. As he arrives in front of the barn, he dismounts his horse and takes it inside. Now inside, he places the horse into one of the stalls. He begins to leave when suddenly he hears a thumping noise coming from the back of the shed. Going toward the sound, he sees in one of the stalls an old African man sitting on the ground, and as he sits there, he tries to catch his breath while pressing a hand on his chest.

"I can't breathe." He looks at Ehmerney and weakly says, "And my heart, it hurts… please… help me!" For a moment, Ehmerney looks at him wide-eyed but then looks away. While looking away, his mind flashes back to an earlier time on the plantation.

A seventeen-year-old Ehmerney comes out of the house. He carries a cloth-covered basket filled with oatmeal raisin cookies. Stepping off the porch, he sees nearby an African male slave chopping wood. With a smile on his face, he heads toward him. "My mother made some freshly baked oatmeal raisin cookies today," he says once standing before the male slave. "Would you like to try one?" The male slave looks at him and then at the cookies. Sensing his hesitation, Ehmerney says, "It's okay. Go ahead… Take one."

The male slave begins to take a cookie but stops when he looks past Ehmerney. "What's wrong?" Ehmerney asks when he sees the look of fear in the male slave's eyes.

Turning to see what the male slave is staring at, Ehmerney sees a middle-aged Caucasian man standing there with an angry look on his face. Once walking towards them, he heatedly says to the male slave, "Git!" And the slave quickly runs away. The middle-aged Caucasian man then harshly rips the basket from Ehmerney's hands. Grabbing him by the arm, he pulls him to the side and says, *"How many times do I have to tell you to stop being kind to the slaves. Stop it, you hear? Do you hear me?"*

"Yes," Ehmerney answers.

"Yes, what?" the middle-aged Caucasian man asks.

"Yes, Father," he answers.

"Help me!" Ehmerney then hears as the flashback comes to an end, "Please, help me!" he hears the old man weakly say as he is now lying down on the ground and reaching out for help.

Kneeling in front of him, Ehmerney sits him up, and after doing so, he looks the old man in the face and says, "You've been here on this plantation for many, many years… but now your time has come to an end." As Ehmerney continues to stare, he sees that the old man is now desperately grasping for breath. His breathing becomes shallow, then… it stops. Once his breathing has stopped, the old man drops his head. Once the man has died, Ehmerney stands to feet. For a second, he looks down at the dead man, then slowly begins walking toward the barn's entrance. He begins to exit when suddenly, he stops and looks to the ground. Inhaling then exhaling, he puts his head up… then leaves.

"Why, God, why?" cries Karina as she sits outside her cabin. With her back leaning up against a tree, she looks toward a navy-blue sky that's filled with silvery clouds and a bright yellow moon.

"Abena," a voice then softly calls her name.

"Mama?" Karina calls as she sits up and looks around with wide eyes. "Is that you?"

"Yes, my daughter."

"It's s-o good to s-ee you tonight, Mama," says Karina. "I need to s-ee you tonight." Karina then burst into tears.

"Oh, Abena," says her mother, Ozigbodi, as she draws close to her. "Why are you crying? What happened to you?" she asks as she sits beside her.

"Mama, today I s-s-saw sum terrible things. Today I s-aw a man get beaten to the point where he barely wa-s living, and I s-aw a woman who-se child was taken away from her and s-old to another s-lave master. Mama, s-eeing those things truly broke my heart."

"So, the tears that you are shedding tonight are not for yourself, but for those around you, who have been treated badly?"

"Yef, I mean yes-s, but how is it that I feel thif way? Why do the pain and s-uffering of others hurt as though it has happened to me?"

"Because you are the type of person who is drawn to other people's pain, Abena. Oh, my daughter, God will use your caring heart to help others."

"But how, Mama? How will God use me so?"

"Quiet your heart, mind, and soul, my daughter," says Ozigbodi as she wipes tears from Karina's face, "and He will show you what to do."

Once her mother finishes talking, she stands to her feet, and as she backs away slowly, she disappears. Now alone, Karina gazes up at the sky once more.

"God," she says aloud as she continues to stare, "thank you for allowing me to experience that vision. Now show me why I feel the way I do." Inhaling and exhaling deeply, Karina stands to her feet and then makes her way into the cabin. Shortly after lying down, she drifts off to sleep. Once asleep, she begins to dream.

Chapter 28

In a dream, Karina finds herself standing in a long hallway with smooth white floors and freshly painted white walls.

"Huh," she gasps as she looks down at her clothing and realizes that she's now wearing a red velvet dress that reaches to the bottom of her feet. "God Almighty," she says as she feels the material, "How can it be that *I* could be wearing s-uch a fancy dre-ss? Only my ma-ster's wife and the other women who come to hi-ss house for tho-se part-ies could wear thif type of dre-ss."

Her attention is then drawn down the hall to a set of white double doors. With caution and even confusion, she begins slowly making her way toward the doors, and as she approaches, she realizes that embedded in each door are rectangular-shaped windows. Now standing in front of the doors, Karina looks above and sees a white sign with black lettering that reads, "The Waiting Room."

Opening one of the doors, Karina finds herself entering a room where the light is dim. However, she is able to see that there are a number of people inside the room, people of various ages, races, and genders.

As she continues to take in the sight, she sees to her left a host of men standing in front of a wall that's papered with pale gold wallpaper. With their backs facing her, they punch holes in the wall with much effort. However, for every hole made, the wall quickly recovers without a trace.

"We're not getting anywhere." A man with bloody knuckles turns to her and angrily says, "We're not getting anywhere! Every day we grind... but for what!" And as if the wall has summoned him, he turns and resumes pounding.

The sudden sound of children crying causes Karina's attention to be shifted to an area in front of her. Looking, Karina sees women sitting in chairs beside one another. The weariness on their faces is complemented with dark circles around their eyes, and sitting in a small chair in front of the women are crying children with fearful looks on their faces. The women try their best to comfort the children through hugs and drying of tears; however, the children's cry persists. "How can we comfort these children when we ourselves need comforting?" one woman asks while looking at Karina.

"Who am I?" Karina suddenly hears a male teenager ask as he steps into her view. "Do you know who I am? If so... please, tell me." He then goes over to a wall and stands with other teenagers who are leaning against a wall that's located to the right of her. As he and the other teenagers lean against the wall, Karina notices that the wall's pale gold wallpaper is peeling in various spots.

"God Almighty," she then says as she looks around the room. "There's such a feeling of hopelessness here."

Suddenly, a hush comes over the room when a set of double wooden doors that are located in the right corner of the room opens. Once the doors open, out steps a middle-aged female wearing an unbuttoned white jacket that reaches to her knees. Complementing the white jacket are a baby blue shirt and pants and white shoes. Hanging around her neck is a silver necklace that has a black narrow tube dangling from it, and at the end of the tube is a shiny silver object that bears a striking resemblance to that of a desk drawer knob.

With the room now completely silent, the middle-aged female stands in the center of the room. She begins to open her mouth to talk but instead puts her head down and sighs.

Raising her head back up, she sighs once more, then utters the words "It doesn't look good." With her spoken words comes a thunder of anguished cries that echo throughout the entire room. With tears now in her own eyes, she begins making her way toward the double wooden doors.

However, just before exiting, Karina interrupts her pace by standing in front of her.

"M-ss," Karina says, "Whatf going on? Whatf going on, M-ss? The men over there are angrily punching hole-s in the wall, the women who look so tired are trying to comfort their children, and the teen-age-rs don't s-eem to know who they are. And now everyone is crying because of what you told them. So whatf going on, M-s? Please… tell me. Who is the person in that room who has these people so upset?"

"It is not a person, Karina."

"No?

"No. It's a feeling… a feeling called hope, and hope is on life support and has been for some time now."

"God Almighty," Karina gasps as she covers her mouth.

"Yes," says the female. "Due to the hardships of life, hope is fading away… and fast." She resumes walking away but stops. "But you!" She then looks at Karina and says, "You can restore hope back to its original glory!"

"Me?" says Karina with a surprised look on her face. "Well, what can I do?"

"Talk to the people, Karina; encourage them to keep believing."

"I-I can't talk to nobody. I'm too s-s-shy, and I can't even peak properly, I mean s-peak."

"You can, Karina. You can do it. God has clothed you in his strength to do so."

"He has?

"Yes!"

"If this why I am clothed in thif fancy red dre-ss?"

"Yes, it's God's way of letting you know that the ministry he has for you will richly bless someone's soul. So, speak to the people, Karina. Speak to them, and in doing so, you will be able to keep hope alive."

As Karina ponders the woman's words, she turns and sees that all the people in the room are now standing directly in front of her, and as they do so, they stand with a look of expectancy on their faces.

A sudden knock at the cabin door later that night causes Karina to wake up. Getting out of bed, she goes toward the door and opens it, and there on the other side stands Virginia.

"Virginia," Karina happily says. "You knocked this ti—" But her words are cut short when she sees Virginia standing there with tears streaming down her face.

"Virginia, what's wrong?"

"My daddy died… someone found him in the barn a little while ago."

"God Almighty. Virginia. I am *so* sorry," Karina tells her as she gives her a hug. "Do you wanna come in and sit for a while?"

"No, Karina, I am on my way to the fire circle, and I stopped by to see if maybe… never mind." Virginia then turns and begins walking away.

"Virginia," Karina then calls to her.

"Yes," she turns and answers.

"I forgot the way to the fire circle, so can I go with you?"

"Alright then… come on."

Moments later, Karina and Virginia arrive at the fire circle. Once there, Karina sees people sitting around the fire with looks of weariness on their faces.

"God Almighty," Karina then says as tears well up in her eyes. "There if s-uch a feeling of hope-less-ness here. I can feel it."

"Every day as a slave is a bad day, Karina… I'm sure you know that." Virginia tells her. "But some days are worse than others, and today is one of those days. For a lot of these slaves, when my Daddy died, so did hope. He was going to speak to them tonight, but now he can't 'cause he gone."

Virginia then sits next to a woman, and as the two of them hug, Virginia cries profusely.

Karina then takes a seat as well, and as she looks at the people around the circle, she sees once more the hurtful expressions on their faces. Suddenly, what the woman told Karina in her dream comes to mind. "Speak to the people, Karina," she recalls hearing the woman say. "Speak to them, and in doing so, you will be able to keep hope alive."

Karina looks to the ground to ponder the thought. She then looks up and says....

Chapter 29

"**I** KNOW YOU ARE HURTING RIGHT NOW… I KNOW YOU are, and I know it s-eems like things in this world are not getting better but worse. Life can be tough," she says as she stands to her feet, "and even cruel. However, you can't allow for the trou-bles of this world to bring you down. You can't allow people who choose to operate in hate to poison your spi-rit. For if so, life and hateful people have won." Going toward the center of the circle, she continues to say, "No matter what hap-pens, in this world or even in this lifetime, make a decision… to keep believing. Keep believing in true happi-ness. Keep believing in love. Keep believing in your dreams, in your faith, in your-self, and yes! Even in God.

"For by doing all of this, we will be able to keep hope alive. Let us *always* do what we can to keep hope alive." Slowly turning in a circle as she talks, she goes on to say, "And let us not only keep hope alive in our own heart-s but also in the heart-s of those around us. S-peak words of encour-agement to your fellow man, pray for one another, believe for and with one another. This belief that we carry—in our hearts, for ourselves, for each other, and even in God—will be the belief that will su-stain us. It will be our burning candle in the mid-st of dark-ness; it will be our shel-ter during a storm. It will be the very thing that will lead *us* and guide us to a better place.

"S-o… I ask everyone tonight who has wit-nessed this mes-sage… Will you keep hope alive… Will you?"

In response to Karina's words, various people around the circle begin to say, "Yes."

"So let'z stand to our feet right now," Karina then says. "Raise our hands in the air," she tells them as she exemplifies, "and give God praise. Even now, even in the midst of all our struggles, even in the mid-st of all our pain, give him praise."

One by one, people begin standing to their feet, and once up, they raise their hands in the air and begin praising God.

Sitting a few feet away from the circle and hunched over on a log is Peter's son Tommy, and as he sits there, he sits shirtless due to the fact that his upper body is still too sore for a shirt. His back is bloody, and pieces of torn skin hang from his shoulders all the way down to his lower back. As he sits there and stares at people praising God, he stares with a bitter look on his face. For a moment, he glances up at the sky… then down at the ground, and as he continues to stare, he says aloud:

"God… Tonight… I sit here with my back in shambles, hurting from the beating I received earlier. But do you wanna know what really hurts tonight, God? It is my spirit. Because of what I been through tonight and even in my life… I don't wanna live anymore, God… I don't wanna live anymore." He shouts toward the sky. "But I can't help but to think on what Karina just said about not allowing people to poison your spirit and that how no matter what may happen in this world or even in this lifetime to keep believing.

"So… because of her words… I *will* keep going, even though everything inside of me is telling me to give up… I will keep going! I will find the strength I need to go on.

"I may have suffered hardships today," he begins to shout, "but I will dare to believe that tomorrow will be a better day. My *back* might be *torn* and my *spirit* might be *bruised*, but *despite*… of how the way…I *feel*… I will give *you* the glory, oh God. I will give you the praise… even now, oh God… even now." Falling to his knees while crying, he lifts his hands in the air and begins praising God.

As Peter's son and the rest of the slaves continue praising God, Ehmerney watches from a distance. He then turns… and walks away.

Chapter 30

HOURS LATER, KARINA ARRIVES BACK AT HER CABIN. once inside, she closes the front door and then presses her back firmly against it. As she stands there, she looks to the floor in deep thought. Raising her hands, she looks and sees that they are shaking. Putting her hand back down, she resumes staring at the floor. "Oooooo!" she then says with glee as she begins twirling around the room. "I did it; I actually did it!" She continues dancing when suddenly she stops and gasps. "Abaven!" she says when she sees him standing there, "I didn't realize you were here."

Without saying a word, Abaven stands in place and looks at her with a raised eyebrow. Noticing his expression, Karina says to him, "Oh, you must think I'm silly dancing around the room like this. I'm just so happy, Abaven. Tonight, for the very first time, I spoke to a crowd of people, and I did not stutter nor did I mispronounce any words." Abaven, still standing there, doesn't utter a sound. "But still," Karina then says as she begins to sit down, "that's no reason for me to be dancing around the room like a silly little girl."

"Ooooo," Abaven then shouts with glee as he draws close to Karina and grabs both hands. "You did it," he exclaims as he begins spinning her around. "You actually did it! You spoke at the fire circle. I knew you could do it, Karina; I knew you could!" Karina and Abaven, now smiling, give each other a hug as they continue dancing around the room.

The next morning, as the calling bell is being rung, Karina walks towards the field with Sarah, Lisa, and Freddy. "That was a mighty fine speech you gave last night, Karina," says Freddy. "But weren't you scared?

"Yes, Freddy, I was scared."

"And you spoke anyway?"

"And how come when you got finished speaking, you asked everyone to stand to their feet and raise their hands in the air... That was too much work," says Lisa.

"Is that why you sat back down?" Karina asks.

"Yep," she replies

As Karina shakes her head and rolls her eyes, Sarah says to her, "Well, thank God for our time at the fire circle. We may not have our freedom, but at least we have that."

"Yes, we do, but freedom is always better," says Karina.

"Oh, now Karina," says Sarah, "don't you go talking about freedom. You know Master doesn't like that. Just be grateful for the fire circle... That's enough."

Just then, an African woman approaches Karina. "Karina?" she calls as she steps into her view.

"Yes," Karina answers.

"Thanks so much for what you said at the fire circle last night," the woman tells her. "Can I give you a hug?'

"Of course," says Karina.

After Karina and the woman embrace, the woman looks at Karina, smiles, and then walks away.

"Wow, that was nice," says Freddy.

"Nice indeed," Karina replies.

Once in the cotton field, Karina finds herself being bombarded by a number of African people who offer compliments and give hugs, and as they continue to do so, Ehmerney stands and watches from the porch. Smoking his cigar, he looks at Karina with a resentful look upon his face.

"Master," Jason suddenly calls as he approaches him. "What's going on with Denise?" he asks as he looks at people embracing her. "Why so many people giving her hugs? What's going on?"

"Denise said something at the fire circle last night, Jason," Ehmerney calmly tells him. "Something about hope."

"Do you think it might cause a problem, Master?"

"It might."

"Do you want me to watch them to make sure it doesn't?"

"No, Jason... that won't be necessary... I'll do it myself. In the mean-time, go break up that love fest, will you?"

"Yes, Master." Ehmerney then hears Jason shout as he begins leaving the porch, "Break that nonsense up and get to work."

Ehmerney, still watching Karina as she begins picking cotton, says in a low tone, "Okay, Denise... okay."

Chapter 31

THAT EVENING, AS KARINA DUMPS THE LAST FILLED BUCKET of cotton into the cart, she hears someone calling from behind. Turning toward the sound of the voice, she sees Peter's son Tommy approaching her. "Hello Karina," he says as he stands before her.

"Tommy, hello," says Karina as she places her bucket on the ground. She attempts to give him a hug, but he quickly moves away.

"Sorry," he then tells her, "Still sore."

"Oh, of course, but how are you?"

"Better, now that I've heard you speak. You helped me, Karina, you really helped me."

"I'm glad that I was able to help you, Tommy. What a shame that you got beaten just for trying to read, though."

"Yeah, it was a shame, and Karina, the book that I was actually trying to read… was the Bible."

"The Bible?"

"Yes, the Bible… He caught me trying to read a verse. But I guess I won't do that anymore. Anyway, Karina, thanks so much for your words."

As Tommy walks away, Karina looks his way. She then looks to the ground to ponder the conversation.

Later that evening, as Karina lies on the wooden bed in her cabin, Tommy's words echo through her mind. "The book that I was actually trying to read… was the Bible," she recalls hearing him say.

Her thoughts then give way to her thinking back to a time in Africa when she, Ruth, Kevin, and her brothers were sitting in front of the fireplace while engaging in nightly devotions.

"So," Ruth then says, "who wants to read from the Bible tonight?"

"I do," cheerfully says Daniel as he raises his hand.

"Okay, Daniel," says Ruth, "And what verse will you be reading from the Bible tonight?"

"Psalms 121, verses 1 through 8."

"Okay, here's the Bible," says Ruth as she prepares to hand it to him.

"No need, Mother," Daniel replies, "I have it memorized." He then says, "Psalms 121, verses 1 through 8: (A Song of degrees.) I will lift up mine eyes unto the hills, from whence cometh my help. My help cometh from the LORD, which made heaven and earth. He will not suffer thy foot to be moved: he that keepeth thee will not slumber. Behold, he that keepeth Israel shall neither slumber nor sleep. The LORD is thy keeper: the LORD is thy shade upon thy right hand. The sun shall not smite thee by day, nor the moon by night. The LORD shall preserve thee from all evil: he shall preserve thy soul. The LORD shall preserve thy going out and thy coming in from this time forth, and even for evermore."

"Very good, Daniel," says Ruth.

"Indeed," says Kevin.

Upon hearing his parents' praise, Daniel smiles with pride. Later, as Daniel sits on the bed in his room, he looks through Ruth's Bible, and as he continues, Karina softly approaches the open door. A light knock causes Daniel to look up. "Oh… Hello, Karina."

"Hello, Daniel. What are you doing?"

"Memorizing more verses."

"Why do you do that?"

"Do what?"

"Memorize verses from the Bible."

"Because of Psalm 119 verse 11: 'Thy word have I hid in mine heart, that I might not sin against thee.' I realize that if I memorize God's word and keep it in my heart and even in my mind, then no one can take it from me."

"Do you think you can help me hide God'z word in my heart?" Karina softly asks.

For a moment, Daniel hesitantly stares at her. He then motions with his head for her to come closer, and when she does, she sits on the bed beside him. Daniel then places Ruth's Bible on her lap and begins teaching her.

As the flashback comes to an end, Karina hears a knock at the cabin door. Opening the door, she sees Virginia standing there. "Hey girl, any chance you coming to the fire circle tonight? Everyone wants to hear you again. There's even more people!"

"Yez," Karina answers as she comes out of the cabin and closes the door behind her, "I mean, yes… I'll come."

As she and Virginia begin walking toward the circle, Karina says to her, "Remember how Peter's son Tommy got whipped for reading... remember?"

"Yes, I remember."

"Do you know what he act-ually got caught reading?"

"What?"

"The Bible."

"What? He got whipped for reading the Bible!?"

"He sure did. He just wanted to learn Bible verses, that's all. But thankz to my brother Daniel for teaching me how to memorize verses, I can now teach others how to do the same so they won't have to try to read it from the book and get in trouble."

"That's great, Karina... just great."

That evening at the fire circle after singing praise songs, Karina teaches the slaves how to memorize Bible verses, and as she does, Ehmerney watches from a distance with a perturbed look on his face.

Chapter 32

THE NEXT DAY, AS EHMERNEY WALKS ONTO THE FRONT porch, he hears singing coming from the field. Looking, he sees three female slaves in the field, picking cotton, and as they continue to do so, they sing a praise song that was sung at the fire circle the previous night. Looking on oddly, he goes back inside the house and into the kitchen. Once there, he sees Isabell baking bread, and as she does so… she sings the exact same praise the other three female slaves were singing. As he stands there and watches in disbelief, Isabell realizes he's looking at her with a look of annoyance. Catching on to his gesture, she stops.

Shaking his head, then rolling his eyes, Ehmerney hastily goes out the back door. Now standing on the back porch, he sees two male slaves emptying out their filled cotton bucket, and as they continue, they sing the same praise song the three female slaves were singing.

Hey!" Ehmerney then shouts, "Stop that singing!" The two men, fearfully looking at him with wide eyes, stop and quickly walk back to the field. Huffing as he shakes his head and rolls his eyes yet again, he walks back into the kitchen. There, he stops, stares at Isabell, then resumes walking toward the front porch. Now on the front porch, he sees Jason approaching him.

"Hello, Master," Jason happily says as he walks onto the porch.

"Hello Jason," Ehmerney gloomily replies.

"What's wrong, Master? You seem upset."

"I *am* upset."

"Why, what's wrong, Master? What's wrong?"

"That Denise got these slaves walking around here singing one of the praise songs they sung at the fire circle last night. I swear, Jason…I swear, if I hear one more person singing that song… they're gonna get it!"

Just then, Mrs. Ehmerney walks onto the front porch. Once there, she begins watering the hanging plants, and while doing so, she sings the same praise that the three female slaves sang.

Upon hearing her singing, Jason looks at Ehmerney with a look of concern

"Jason," Ehmerney then annoyingly says

"Yes, Master," he fearfully answers

"Gather all the slaves together for a meeting."

Moments later, the slaves gather in front of the house with Karina, Sarah, Freddy, and Lisa standing in the front. As they continue to stand, they see Ehmerney walking from inside the house and onto the porch. Once there, Jason stands beside him.

"Everyone... Listen," Ehmerney then says with a big commanding voice.

"Yeah, listen," says Jason with his hands on his hips.

"It has come to my attention that there has been singing going on today, singing that has interrupted the flow of work, and the songs that slaves were singing was songs they got from the fire circle last night. Well, as of today, that is going to stop."

"Yeah," says Jason, "it's gonna stop."

"No more singing," says Ehmerney.

"No more singing," Jason repeats.

"And no more fire circle."

"Yeah, that's right," says Jason. "No more fire circle, y'all."

"Jason?" Ehmerney then calmly but infuriatingly says.

"Yes, Master?" he answers with a smile.

"Shut up."

"Yes, Master," he responds with a glazed look in his eyes.

"So, like I said, no more singing and no more fire circle. Anyone who participates in either of these things shall be severely punished... Now get back to work!"

"I'm sorry, Karina," says Sarah as everyone begins to disperse.

"Me too, Karina. I'm so sorry," says Freddy.

"What are we going to do now, Karina?" Lisa asks.

"I don't know," Karina answers. "I don't know what I'm going to do now."

With a sorrowful look in their eyes, Sarah, Freddy, and Lisa walk away. Looking to the ground, Karina inhales then exhales. She begins walking away when suddenly Jason calls.

"Denise!" Turning toward him, she sees him leaving the porch and approaching her. "So, it looks like your little plans to talk to the slaves about hope have failed. No more singing and no more fire circle. No more, Denise... It's over. Your plans have been defeated." He begins walking away when suddenly he stops, "Hey...wait a minute." He then says, "I just came up with a clever nickname for you... Defeated... Defeated Denise." Laughing loudly, Jason resumes walking away.

Karina, now standing alone, stands with tears in her eyes. She sighs deeply and then returns to the field.

Chapter 33

TWELVE YEARS LATER ON A FALL MORNING OF SEPTEMBER 23, 1823, a now thirty-one-year-old Karina leaves her cabin. She begins walking toward the field but stops and looks toward the path that leads to the fire circle. Moments later, Karina arrives at the circle. There, she sees old burnt logs, and among the logs are now tall weeds that have grown up in between them. As she stares at the disheartening sight, she says aloud, "Maybe Jason was right... Maybe I am Defeated Denise after all."

"Not so, Abena," she suddenly hears a man say. "Not so!" Turning toward the voice, she sees Donkor standing there.

"Papa," Karina says as she experiences a vision of him. "You are here."

"I am... I am always here with you... Even when you don't see me... still, I am here. You feel defeated right now, but I say to you, not so. People will try their best to defeat you, and for a while, it may seem like they won. Just like with me, your family, and your village, people try their best to defeat us, and it seemed like they won, but what they didn't realize was what lay beneath."

Donkor then goes and moves one of the old burnt logs from the fire pit, and when he does, Karina sees a bright yellow flower that has grown underneath. Donkor then picks the flower, walks over to Karina, and places it in the corner of her hair, and as he holds her close, he tells her, "What you might think is dead is not really dead, daughter. In life, we experience battles and we might even lose those battles, but as a child of God... we never lose the war. God has given you a ministry, a ministry that is far from over, no matter what things may look like... It's not over. In fact, starting today, you will cross paths with someone who will need to hear a word from you."

"Who?"

"Well, I can't tell you that. If so, it would ruin the surprise," he says with a smile. "But stay encouraged, daughter... Oh, and one more thing before I leave."

"What?"

"Happy Day of your Birth."

As she renders a smile, Donkor hugs her, then kisses her on the forehead. He then slowly backs away and vanishes.

Karina, now alone, stares at the fire pit once more, and as she stares, she breathes a sigh of relief, then smiles. Suddenly, she hears the bell being rung. Turning toward the sound, she puts her head up and begins making her way toward the field.

Chapter 34

HOURS LATER, AS KARINA PICKS COTTON, EHMERNEY walks onto the front porch, and while standing there, he looks at the slaves in the field. His eyes then lay hold of Karina, and as he looks at her with the yellow flower in her hair, his mouth as well as his eyes open wide. As he continues to stare, his mind flashes back to an earlier time on the plantation when he was eighteen years of age.

While standing in the barn, Ehmerney remembers holding a yellow flower in his hand. He remembers giving the flower to someone. He recalls standing before a dark-skinned African female who, after receiving the flower, places it in her hair. As Ehmerney and the dark-skinned female stand before each other, they stare deeply into each other's eyes. Suddenly, the barn door opens, causing Ehmerney and the female to look with fear.

As the flower in Karina's hair continues to hold Ehmerney's attention, he recalls standing on the porch and watching as his father lifts the now crying African female up off the ground and into the back of the wagon. Once chaining her to a pole that's station on the cart's rim, he orders for the wagon to go, and as it rides off, she cries out, "Richard... Richard."

"Don't move." Ehmerney's father then looks at him and says, "Don't you dare come off that porch."

Ehmerney looks on with tears in his eyes. However, due to his father's command, he remains on the porch. His father then walks onto the porch. Once there, he stops and meanly stares at him. "Richard," he then harshly says, "in the house now... We need to talk." At that moment, he begins walking inside, and as he does, Ehmerney fearfully stares in his direction.

"Jason!" Ehmerney then shouts as the flashback comes to an end. "Jason!"

"Yes, Master," he comes to the stairs and answers.

"Look at Denise!"

Jason turns and looks at her.

"You go tell that Denise to get that ridiculous flower out of her hair."

"Yes, Master." Jason then quickly approaches Karina. There he says, "Hey, Denise, what you think you're doing? You get that flower outta your hair."

Ehmerney continues to look on with anger, when suddenly he sees a wagon hastily riding onto the property. As the wagon draws closer to the house, Ehmerney notices there's a muscular African man seated in the back. Now in front of the house, the wagon comes to a complete stop. Ehmerney, walking off the porch and toward the wagon, realizes that the African man's hands and feet are bound together with thick rope, and on his head is an iron device. The device the man wears consists of a thin metal bar that extends from the back of his head to the bottom of his nose, with a large metal piece that covers his mouth. Holding the mouthpiece and thin bar together are two thin bars that are stationed on each side of the mask. The driver of the wagon is a Caucasian man in his sixties. The passenger is a Caucasian man in his twenties. After stepping out of the wagon, the man in his twenties draws close to the man in his sixties and whispers, "Pa, I'm glad you were able to talk Mr. Ehmerney into taking him... This slave is wild."

"Yeah, he is, but if anyone can control him, it's definitely Ehmerney. He's the best slave master around."

"Does he know how wild and crazy this slave gets?"

"Shhh," the man in his sixties says to his son when he sees Ehmerney walking toward them. "Hello, Richard," the man in his sixties then says with a smile. "How are you doing today?"

"I am well; how are you?"

"Good. Thanks for being willing to take this slave."

"A pleasure to help. Just wondering why, you chose to let him go for free... Is there anything wrong with him?"

"There's nothing wrong with him, Richard, nothing at all. He's in perfect condition."

"Then why is he wearing a metal muzzle?"

"Because... because," the man in his sixties tries to come up with an answer as he looks to the ground.

"Because he's really hungry and he hasn't eaten yet," the man in his twenties quickly interjects. "We didn't want him to mistakenly bite your hand."

"So, he bites people's hands when he hasn't eaten?"

"Oh, no," says the man in his sixties. "Youngster is just jesting with you. He's actually wearing that muzzle to ensure safe delivery."

"Okay," Ehmerney says with a skeptical look on his face. "Well, let's get him out of the wagon." Ehmerney then snaps his finger four times, and upon him doing so, out come four strong-looking African men running toward the wagon.

"Yes, Master!" They all simultaneously say when they arrive.

"We got a new slave today. Get him out of the wagon and stand him up."

The four men pull the male slave out of the wagon. Once out, they stand him to his feet. "Oh wow," says Ehmerney as he stares, "This new slave is taller than me and looks strong."

"Yes, he's very tall," says the man in his sixties, "and very strong... But you're still gonna take him, right?"

"Yes, I'll take him."

"Great! Come on," the man in his sixties then whispers to his son. "Let's hurry up and get outta here before he changes his mind."

Ehmerney looks the bound slave up and down. "Can't I at least give you guys somethi—" Ehmerney then turns to the man and his son to say, but he stops talking when he only sees a trail of dust they leave behind as they quickly ride off the property. "Okay," Ehmerney then says as he refaces the slave.

Karina, looking on from a distance, finds herself fixated on the slave's appearance. "Why does that man look so familiar to me?" she asks aloud.

Karina then hears Ehmerney tell the four men, "Remove the iron muzzle from off his head so I can get a good look at him."

Once the men remove the muzzle from the man's face, Karina gasps. "God Almighty," she then says as she covers her mouth. "That man is...."

Chapter 35

EHMERNEY THEN SAYS TO THE MEN, "NOW TAKE OFF THE ropes."

The African men loosen the ropes from around the slave's hands and feet. Once the last rope is taken off... the slave lunges at Ehmerney. As he tightly wraps both hands around his neck, he pins Ehmerney to the ground.

The four men manage to pull the slave off and away from him. However, once they have the slave in their possession, they are tossed to the side like old rag dolls. Now free of their clutch, the slave lunges at Ehmerney once more, this time grabbing him by the shirt. He prepares to punch Ehmerney in the face when suddenly, he hears "Emmanuel!" Looking up, he sees Karina standing there.

"Karina?" the slave answers while staring wide-eyed. "Is that really you?"

"Yes, Emmanuel, it's me."

Suddenly, the four men grab Emmanuel from behind. "Take him to that tree and tie him there," Ehmerney angrily says as he stands to his feet. "And make sure his back is facing me." As Ehmerney continues to regain his composure, his wife and his son come running to his side.

"Richard, oh my God. We just saw what happened. Are you okay?" his wife asks.

"I'm fine, Martha."

"That slave nearly killed you," his son Johnathan says.

"Yes, he did. That slave is crazy. Son, make me a promise."

"Yes, Father, what is it?"

"If you ever see this slave, or any, lunge at me like that... shoot them dead."

"Yes, Father, I will."

"Now bring me my whip!"

Once Ehmerney receives his whip, he walks toward the tree where Emmanuel is positioned. Now at the tree, Ehmerney rips the shirt from Emmanuel's back. "You foolish, foolish slave," he then tells him. "You gonna learn to respect me." Ehmerney begins whipping Emmanuel. However, the slave does not scream out. Instead, he just angrily looks away. As Karina continues to witness the horror of seeing her brother getting whipped, tears well up in her eyes.

Chapter 36

LATE THAT AFTERNOON, AS KARINA STANDS OUTSIDE HER cabin, she paces back and forth. Suddenly, she sees the four African men carrying a now physically exhausted Emmanuel by the arms and legs. As they continue to do so, Ehmerney follows behind. "Drop him over there," Ehmerney then says to the men. Hearing the command, they head over to a cabin that's across from Karina's, then drop him on the ground and deliberately on his back.

"Ahhhhh," Emmanuel screams as his bloody and bruised back hits the cold, hard ground

"Now what do you want us to do with him?" one of the men asks.

"Just let him be," says Ehmerney. "That whipping he received should keep him calm for the rest of the day and even the night."

"I hope so," another one of the men then says. "He sure is stubborn. You had to beat him several times just for him to finally break."

"I would have beaten him more, but my whip kept getting caught in his hairy back," says Ehmerney. "In fact, that's what I'll call him... I'll call him Harry. You hear that?" he then shouts to Emmanuel as he's still lying unconscious on the ground. "Your new name is Harry. Come on, men," Ehmerney then says, "Let's go."

Once Ehmerney and the rest of the men have left, Karina discreetly goes over to where Emmanuel is lying. "Emmanuel," she then calls as she kneels beside him and lightly touches him. Emmanuel opens his eyes and looks at her but doesn't say a word. "Let me take you to my cabin so I can nurse your back. Can you stand?" Emmanuel tries to stand but struggles. Noticing his hardship, Karina helps him up. Once up, they both slowly but surely make their way to Karina's cabin.

Moments later, as Emmanuel sits in a wooden chair with his back exposed, Karina scoops with her fingers a thick, greasy ointment from a small jar she holds in her hands. "I'm grateful to my friend Sarah for having this ointment."

"Yeah," Emmanuel says gloomily while sitting hunched over in the chair. With her fingers, Karina adds the ointment to Emmanuel's back. "Ahhhhh," he screams and moves when she does so.

"Oh, I'm sorry... Does that hurt?"

"No, Karina," he sarcastically tells her. "It doesn't hurt."

"I see you're still oh so kind, Emmanuel."

"I try my best."

"And still very sarcastic. Mother and Father never liked that about you, especially Father. It used to drive him mad."

"I'm just in a lot of pain, Karina, okay?"

"I know you're in a lot of pain, Emmanuel, and I'm trying to help."

"Well, can you be just a little gentler in your help?"

"Well, I don't know... Can you be a lot nicer?"

Sighing, he responds, "I can do that. Hmm." He then laughs.

"What... what's so funny

"Look at us sitting here having an argument even though we haven't seen each other in years."

"Amazing, isn't it?" says Karina as she begins to laugh as well. "Like we never skip a beat."

"Actually, we have. You never used to argue back. Whenever someone said something you didn't like, you would just run away and cry. Now look at you," he says as he turns and faces her. "You're sitting here... busting my chops... I'm so proud."

"Well, like Father always said: What doesn't kill you makes you stronger, and slavery hasn't killed me, so I guess it brought out the fighter in me."

"It has," he says as he faces forward. "Oh, and another thing I notice about you," he says as he turns back around to face her.

"What?"

"You don't stutter anymore, and you even speak properly."

"I don't stutter anymore, Emmanuel, and I used to have a hard time saying words clearly, especially words that begin with an S. But not anymore, <u>soooo</u>, *shut up*, turn around and let me *fin-ish* nursing your back."

"Yes, ma'am," Emmanuel says with laughter as he faces forward. "But please, Sis... add the ointment carefully... *please*."

"Okay... Emmanuel?"

"Yes, Sis."

"It's soooo very good to see you again."

"And you as well. Have you seen the others?"

"Well, when I first arrived here in South Carolina, I saw Victor as he was getting auctioned off. But after that, I didn't see him no more, nor the others. How about you... Did you see any of them?"

"No... I haven't. So much has happened since we got here, Emmanuel."

"Yes, so much."

"So how did you wind up here anyway?"

"Oh, by being my normal charming self to all my masters."

"Masters... How many masters did you have?"

"Six."

"Six?"

"Yep. In fact, the master on this plantation is my seventh one. They couldn't control me, Karina," Emmanuel says with a smirk. "They couldn't control me... That's why they had to get rid of me. They couldn't control me, and I wasn't going to let them. Even when I first got here on this plantation and saw that slave master standing before me, I swear, I was going to kill that no good son of a..."

"Emmanuel!" Karina interjects, "Your language!"

"Well, I was, Karina. I would kill all of them if I could."

"Emmanuel, you always had your temper, but you never talked about killing someone."

"You're not the only person slavery has changed."

"Slavery may have taken a toll on my body, Emmanuel... but I refused to allow it to have my heart, my mind, and my spirit."

"Then you're a better person than me."

"No Emmanuel... no... I refuse to believe that. You are still a good person... You're the same big brother who took up for me whenever someone would mess with me. You're still that same person... You're just hurting. But you're here now, and we're together, so we can help each other through this, okay?"

"Are you finished applying the ointment?"

"I am."

"Okay," Emmanuel then says as he abruptly gets up from the chair. "Thanks for helping me, and see you tomorrow," he adds as he begins heading toward the door. Karina, standing up as well, follows him. Opening the door, Emmanuel begins to exit, but Karina stops him.

"Try to get some rest tonight, okay?"

Smiling a little, Emmanuel looks at her and says, "Okay, Sis, I will." He then kisses her on the cheek and leaves.

After exiting the room, Karina goes and sits in the chair, and for a moment, she stares at the floor to ponder the interaction. "Oh, dear God," she then looks toward the ceiling and prays. "I know you brought my brother Emmanuel here so I can minister to him. Just tell me what to say." After praying, Karina gets in bed and goes to sleep.

Chapter 37

THE NEXT MORNING, AS EMMANUEL SITS OUTSIDE HIS cabin, he looks to the ground in deep thought. "You always had your temper," he recalls hearing Karina say the night before. He then finds himself reminiscing about a moment he had with Kevin while sitting in front of the fireplace at the cabin in Africa. "You always seem so angry, Emmanuel," he remembers hearing Kevin say. "Why are you so angry? Tell me."

Emmanuel's thoughts then lead back to a time when he saw his birth father. Emmanuel, a nine-year-old boy, stands inside his hut in the African village, and as he looks a few feet ahead of him, he sees a very tall and superiorly muscular African man standing in the hut's doorway with his back facing him. Emmanuel then runs up to the man.

"Father," he gleefully says as he stands beside him and hugs him by the waist. Receiving his embrace, his father looks down at him and smiles as he drapes an arm around his shoulder. Emmanuel then recalls the times his father lifted him in the air by pushing him up with his powerful arms. He also remembers the time his father carried him and his three younger brothers on his back while walking throughout the village.

As Emmanuel continues to reminisce on such sweet moments with his father, a light smile graces his face. But the smile dissipates when he suddenly remembers the day his village was attacked. Emmanuel remembers, while intruders attack his village, he, his mom, and his three younger brothers fleeing for safety. As they continue to run, a net is cast over his mother. "Mama," Emmanuel cries out when he sees that she has been captured.

He attempts to free her, but his mother says, "No... No! Go... I need you to keep your brothers safe. Go!"

With tears in his eyes, Emmanuel takes hold of his younger brothers' hands and begins running away. He continues running with his brothers, when suddenly he sees a large, thick bush. "There!" he shouts. "Let's hide there." Emmanuel and his brothers hide inside the bush. Once there, Emmanuel looks through an opening and sees his father. With a spear in his hand, he fights off the intruders, but suddenly, a dozen Caucasian soldiers with swords and guns surround him.

"You're totally surrounded now," one of the soldiers says, "so drop your weapon and surrender." With the spear still clenched tightly in his hand, Emmanuel sees his father looking around the circle. He then drops the spear to the ground, gets on his knees, and raises both hands in the air. Emmanuel looks on in disbelief. A sudden cry from his youngest brother causes Emmanuel to look away, and once doing so, he takes hold of his youngest brother as well as the other two. As he continues to hold them close, he blankly stares directly in front of him, and while doing so, he begins to develop an angry look on his face as tears begin to fall silently from his eyes.

"Good morning, Emmanuel," he suddenly hears Karina say, interrupting his flashback.

"Good morning, Karina," he answers. As he stands to his feet, he quickly wipes away the tears that were developing in his eyes.

"How long have you been up?"

"Never really slept, actually. Because of my back, I've been tossing and turning all night, and these wooden beds sure don't help."

"Oh, I'm sorry."

"It's okay, Sis. It's not your fault."

"Your eyes… They're watery. Why do they look that way?" Karina then asks.

"It's just because I'm tired."

Just then, they hear a bell being rung.

"What's that bell for?" Emmanuel then asks.

"Oh, that's the bell telling us to report to the field so we can begin our day of labor."

"Really," Emmanuel suddenly says with a plastered smile on his. "I'm so excited," he adds as he begins jumping up and down.

Shaking her head, then rolling her eyes, Karina says with a light laugh, "Come on, Mr. Excited. Let's head to the field."

As Karina and Emmanuel walk toward the bell, they see Jason ringing it.

Stopping, he says, "Well, look who it is: Denise, Denise, Denise. How you doing today, Denise?"

"Denise?" Emmanuel questions as he and Karina stop to talk to Jason. "Who's Denise?"

"I'm Denise. That's the name they gave me."

"And you answer to that?"

"Yeah, she does," Jason interjects. "And she better… if she knows what's good for her."

"And who are you supposed to be?" Emmanuel then says to Jason. "The welcome committee?"

"I'm Mr. Jason," he says as he places his hands on his hips and sticks his lips out. "And I'm in charge of this plantation here, and Mr. Jason doesn't take no stuff from nobody." As Jason introduces himself to Emmanuel, Karina stands behind him and mimics his actions. Emmanuel, noticing, begins to laugh

"What?" Jason then asks when he sees Emmanuel grinning. "What are you laughing at?"

"Oh, nothing," Emmanuel quickly answers.

Jason looks behind him to see what Emmanuel could be laughing at, only to see Karina standing while looking the other way.

"Jason!" Ehmerney suddenly calls from the porch.

"Yes, Master!" he answers after running onto the porch.

"I see you met the new slave."

"Yes, Master, I have."

"Well, I want you to work closely with him today and keep a good eye on him. For some odd, crazy reason, this slave seems to have a lot of pent-up aggression. Take him to the woodpile and let him chop wood. That should help absorb some of that energy, and let me know if you have any problems."

"Yes, Master, I will." Jason begins leaving the porch but stops. "What is his name, Master?" he asks.

"Harry. His name is Harry."

"Harry, got it."

Seconds later, Jason returns to Karina and Emmanuel. Now standing before them, he says, "Alright, Denise, you get your bucket and head out to the field. Harry, you come with me."

"Harry, huh? So, that's my name now?"

"Yeah, it is! Now come wit me."

As Jason leads the way, Emmanuel notices that he's stomping the ground with his head up and chest out. Emmanuel, watching from behind, begins mimicking his walk.

"Okay, here we go," says Jason once he and Emmanuel reach a large pile of tree logs. "Master wants you to cut these logs down to size so they can be used for the fireplace inside his house. Here," Jason then says as he hands him an axe, "Get started, and don't stop till I tell you to... You hear?"

"Okay," says Emmanuel as he takes the axe.

"Okay, what?"

"Okay... I hear you."

"No, you suppose to say my name."

"Okay... Jason?"

"No, it's Mr. Jason," he demands as he stomps a foot.

"Jason," Emmanuel responds as he begins positioning himself to cut the wood.

"Mr. Jason!" he says as his voice begins to rise.

"Jason," Emmanuel says once more.

"No!" he then screams. "It's *Mr.* Jasonnnn!" he shouts at the top of his lungs as he jumps up and down.

For a second, Emmanuel gives no reply. Then he says, "Jason."

"You're being rebellious... I'm telling Master."

As Jason leaves to go get Ehmerney, Emmanuel stares with a smirk. Seconds later, Jason returns with Ehmerney. "He's giving me trouble already Master," Jason tells Ehmerney as he and Ehmerney look at Emmanuel. "He won't say my name right."

"Harry," Ehmerney then shouts to Emmanuel as he draws close to him. "Listen to Jason!"

"It's Mr. Jason," Jason softly corrects.

"Whatever!" Ehmerney responds. "Listen to him," he then says to Emmanuel. "If you disrespect him, you disrespect me. Got it!?"

"Yes, Master."

With an angry look on his face, Ehmerney walks away. Once he has departed, Emmanuel begins chopping wood, and as he does, he does it with a smirk on his face. "I see that smirk," Jason then says to him. "Trying to be slick with not saying my name right, huh? You're just jealous."

"Jealous... of what?" Emmanuel stops and asks with a look of disbelief.

Chapter 37

"Jealous that I work with the Master. That's why you being hateful. In fact, that's what I'm going to start calling you from now on... Hateful Harry."

"First off, my name is Emmanuel, not no *damn* Harry. And secondly, I am not jealous of you... at all. I actually think what you are doing is sad. Helping a white man to control us. You oughta be ashamed of yourself."

"Well, I'm not. Someone needs to control y'all crazy ass n****."

"N***?! Did you just call n****? How you gonna stand there and call us that? You one of us!"

"No, I'm not. I work directly with the Master, so I'm better than you."

"Oh, you are, aren't you?" Emmanuel responds with laughter. "Well, make sure you tell yourself that tonight when it's time to go to sleep, so that way when you *do* lie down, you can get a good night's rest."

"I am better than you."

"Okay, Jason... Oh, I'm sorry... what I should have said was ...Mr. ... Jasonnn," Emmanuel says as he mockingly jumps up and down. "How was that?" he then looks at Jason and says with a smile, "Did I get it right this time?"

"Oh, you think you so funny, don't you?" Jason asks him as he sees Emmanuel laugh a little. "Yeah, I know your type. You're the type of n*** that always gotta have something smart to say."

"And you're the type of guy that always got to _act big_ in order to make up for what he doesn't have below."

Upon hearing Emmanuel's words... tears begin to well up in Jason's eyes. "Master!" he then shouts. "Master! ... I'm ma tell Master... I'm ma tell Master on you," he whines as he walks away.

"Fine, Jason! Go tell Master... little rat," he then says underneath his breath.

"Again, Harry!?" Ehmerney then says as he shows up on the scene. "You're giving Jason trouble again? Stop giving him... Wait." He then looks at Jason and says, "Are you crying?"

"No," Jason sorrowfully responds.

"Well... listen to Jason, you hear? If I have to come over here one more time, you're gonna get it. You hear me, Harry. You hear me?"

"Yes, Master," Emmanuel says with a smirk. "Master?"

"What?"

"May I please go and get a drink of water?"

"Go! And make it quick!"

"Yes, Master." As Emmanuel goes to get a drink of water, he glances at Jason with a smile.

Now at the water station, Emmanuel drinks as Karina suddenly comes beside him. "I see you over there with Jason," she says to him.

"Oh, you're seeing that, huh?"

"Yes, I am. Why, Emmanuel? Why must you cause trouble?"

"Well, sorry Sis, but I'm not like you. Sorry I'm not okay with being a slave."

"I'm not okay with being a slave either," Karina angrily rebuts with her hands on her hips. "I just learn how to pick and choose my battles. Sometimes we have to be willing to lose the battle in order to win the war, Emmanuel. Life as a slave is hard enough. Why make it worse?"

Sighing, Emmanuel says, "Okay, Karina… okay. Perhaps, you're right. I will try my best to control my temper… and my mouth, so I can at least have a good day."

"Good. Well, we have to get back to work. Try to have a good day, Emmanuel… please," Karina tells him as she gives him a hug.

"I'll try," Emmanuel replies as he hugs her as well.

Minutes later, Emmanuel returns to the log pile, and as he begins chopping wood, Jason approaches him from behind. "Hey, Harry," Jason then says. "Why was you over there hugging Denise?"

"Who?" Emmanuel stops and asks.

"You know, Denise!"

Upon hearing the inquiry, Emmanuel confusedly looks to the side. "Oh, that's right," he then says. "I forgot… her name is Denise."

"That's right. So why was you hugging her?"

"Well, *Denise* is my sister, Jason, and she and I was just giving each other a brotherly and sisterly hug."

"Oh, well, that's good. At first I thought you was trying to get with her."

"What? No, I'm definitely not trying to do that."

"Well, good, 'cause I've been looking at her lately, and she's been look-ing mighty fine."

Hearing Jason's comment, Emmanuel stops and stares down at the wood.

"You know, when she first came here, she was an itty-bitty thing, but now that she's gotten older, her breast has gotten larger, her hips… wider, yeah, she's looking mighty fine these days. Oh, I'm sorry. Here I am standing here and going on and on and on about how good your sister looks when I haven't even asked how you felt about it, Harry. So..." Jason then goes beside him and looks at him with a smirk. "How do you feel about it, Harry? How do you feel about me talking about your sister?"

As Ehmerney sits on the porch, he smokes a cigar. Suddenly, he hears, "Ahhhh!"

"What the devil," he shouts as he jumps up from his seat. Running off the porch and toward the sound, he sees Jason lying on the ground while crying, and standing over top of him is Emmanuel with a grin.

"Harry!" Ehmerney calls as Emmanuel suddenly looks at him with wide eyes.

"What did you do to Jason? Why is he lying on the ground crying? What did you do to him?"

"...I mistakenly kicked him."

"You, *mis-takenly* kicked him!? And where on Earth did you mistakenly kick him at Harry... in his chest?"

"No," he lightly answers. "Not his chest... lower."

"His stomach?"

"Lower."

"...His knees?"

"Higher."

"Harry... You kicked him there? How on Earth did you mistakenly kick him there?"

Emmanuel begins to talk, but Ehmerney interjects.

"And before you explain, you better have a good reason, or else you're gonna get a good whipping. Now, how did you kick him there?"

"Well," Emmanuel then says, "I had a cramp in my leg... and I was stretching out my leg to get rid of the cramp... and while I was doing that... that's when I mistakenly kicked him."

Noticing the look of disbelief on Ehmerney's face, Emmanuel goes toward a tree and assumes the position to get beaten.

Moments later, a wagon rides onto the property, and seated in the driver's seat is Ehmerney's son Johnathan with his wife in the passenger seat. As the wagon stops in front of the house, Ehmerney approaches with a whip still in hand. "Richard, darling, hello," says Mrs. Ehmerney as Ehmerney helps her down from the wagon.

"How did everything go while in town?" Ehmerney asks.

"Great! The dishes that I ordered for our party came in today. "What's wrong?" she then asks when she notices a perturbed look on his face.

"Oh, it's just that new slave."

"Is he still giving you trouble?"

"Still giving me trouble, and I swear, Jason is no help. Those two together are like children."

"Well, maybe you can get that new slave away from Jason for a while and have him help me with taking these crates of dishes into the house."

"That sounds like a good idea."

Back at the woodpile, as Emmanuel cuts wood, Jason walks up behind him, and as he folds his arms, he looks at Emmanuel and says, "Soooo, now that we have gotten beaten, how do we feel?"

"Oh, I feel great!" Emmanuel quickly replies.

"Well, maybe I should tell Master to give you another one."

"Go ahead, tell him. I don't care. I'm used to getting beaten."

Jason begins stomping his way toward Ehmerney's house but stops when he suddenly sees Ehmerney walking toward him.

"He's doing it again, Master!" Jason tries to tell him. "He's starting trouble again!"

"Not now, Jason!" Ehmerney interjects while facing a hand toward his face. "Harry! You come with me. I have another task for you to do."

"Oh, master," Emmanuel then sarcastically says in a sad tone, "can I stay here with Jason? Can I… *please!*"

"No," Ehmerney tells him. "Come with me!"

"Yes, Master," says Emmanuel. As he begins walking away with Ehmerney, Emmanuel discreetly looks at Jason with a sneer.

Jason, noticing, begins sulking.

Now in front of the house, Emmanuel sees a wagon that has five fairly-sized wood crates sitting in the back. "Harry," Ehmerney then tells him, "I want you to take these crates out of the wagon and bring them into the house through the back door and only through the back door. You hear?"

"Yes, Master."

An hour later, Emmanuel brings the last crate into the back kitchen. He begins to place the crate on the floor when suddenly the bottom of the crate breaks, allowing two dishes to fall out. However, just before the dishes hit the floor, Emmanuel quickly grabs them. After placing the two dishes on a nearby table, Emmanuel carefully places the broken box on the floor. He then picks up the two dishes to put them on top of the box.

However, just before doing so, Mrs. Ehmerney enters the kitchen. *"Oh my God!"* she shouts. *"Get your dirty hands off my dishes!"*

"They almost fell, and I was just trying to save them."

"Put them down, I tell you. Put them down now!"

"What's all the fuss?" Ehmerney says as he comes running into the kitchen.

"This slave had his dirty hands all over our dishes. I need to replace the dishes now," Mrs. Ehmerney begins to whine, "because those dishes are ruined."

"They're not ruined," says Emmanuel as he looks at her oddly. "Just wash them off with some soapy water… They'll be okay."

"Get out!" Mrs. Ehmerney then tells him. *"Put the dishes down and get out… Get out!"*

With a glazed look now in his eyes, Emmanuel puts the dishes on a counter and begins leaving the kitchen. However, just before exiting, he hears Mrs. Ehmerney say, "He's no good for anything, isn't he?"

Now outside, Karina approaches him.

"Hello, Emmanuel," she then says with a smile. "How was the rest of your day?"

Emmanuel, standing there, looks to the ground but gives no reply.

"Emmanuel?" Karina calls as she tries to look him in the face.

Suddenly… Emmanuel takes off running toward the wooded area of the plantation.

"Emmanuel?" Karina calls confusedly as she watches him run away.

Chapter 38

THAT EVENING, AS RAIN POUNDS HEAVILY ON THE ROOF OF Karina's cabin, Karina stands inside, pacing the floor. "Where is he?" she says while pacing. She then goes to the door, opens it, and looks out. Closing the door, she looks to the floor and sighs. Suddenly, a hard knock is heard at the door. Opening it, she sees Emmanuel standing on the other side... soaking wet. "Oh my god, Emmanuel, don't just stand there; get in here." Once inside, Karina takes the blanket off her bed and begins drying him off, but Emmanuel pushes the blanket away. "You had me worried sick. Where did you run off to?"

"I don't even remember. I just kept running and running till I couldn't run no more. Then it started to rain, and by then I was too tired to move, so I just laid there and got wet."

"What on Earth happened that made you run off like that?"

"Oh, nothing major, Just the usual... oppression."

"But something bad must have really happened... Was it Jason again? He can be a lot to deal with."

"No, Sis, it wasn't that damn Jason this time. It was the master's wife. She was the one who pissed me off."

"What did she do?"

"I was taking crates from the wagon, crates filled with dishes. I was taking them into the house when one of the boxes broke, but before the dishes could hit the floor, I saved them so they wouldn't fall on the floor and break."

"Well, that was good."

"Wasn't though, because when she came into that kitchen and saw me standing there holding the plates, she began screaming and hollering. And you know what she even said to me... You know what that mean devil lady said to me?"

"What?"

Emmanuel begins to tell her but stops. He then says, "She said get your dirty hands off my dishes."

"Oh, Emmanuel."

"And what's worse, she said her dishes are now ruined, all because I touched them. I tell you, Karina. What type of life we have where we not only get treated like cattle but also like we're some kind of disease?"

"I know, Brother," Karina says as she gives him a hug

"Do you?" he tells her as he moves away. "Because you seem to be walking around here like you're on some kind of a fancy trip *Denise*."

"Please don't call me that."

"Well, that's your name, isn't it? Denise... Denise, Denise, Denise," he adds in a mocking tone.

"Oh, Emmanuel, I know you're hurting right now. And believe me, I had those moments of anger and rage myself, so I know how you feel."

"Do you?"

"I do!"

"Well, tell me this, Sis... Have you ever seen God surrender? What?

"Have you ever... seen... God... surrender? Have you?"

"No... I haven't."

"Well, I did... I saw God surrender... I saw him bow down to the devil."

"You did?"

"I did... My father. He was a mighty, mighty man. He seemed like a giant, so tall and strong, it was as though he could do anything and do no wrong. But then one day, when our village got attacked and me and my brothers was hiding in the bushes for safety... I saw him... I saw that when the white men surrounded him with their guns and swords, he dropped his spear to the ground, got on his knees, raised his hands in the air... and surrendered."

"Oh, Emmanuel."

"And even though I was mad at the white men who took him captive, I was ten times angrier at him for surrendering. He wasn't supposed to surrender, Karina. He wasn't supposed to do that; not him, not my father, not a man who was like a God to me. And ever since I witnessed that horrible, horrible sight, I made a vow to myself that I will never do what he did. And you know what, Karina? I've kept my word... It's been years now and still... I bow to no one. Many masters have tried to control me, but they *all* failed.

I bow to no one, but even though I refused to bow… *still* they have found a way to take something from me, something that was truly precious and priceless. More priceless than my land, more priceless than my freedom, even more priceless than my family."

"What in the world could possibly be more priceless than those things, Emmanuel?"

"My manhood. Karina, you might know what it feels like to be a slave, but do you know what it feels like to be a man… Do you? Do you know what it feels like to spend your life trying to find out what a real man is supposed to *look like, act like, be like*? Just so when you finally find it, it gets stripped away… Do you know what that feels like, Karina… Do you? At the end of the day, when all is said and done… all a man has left is his dignity. That's all he has left, Karina. That's all he has left… is his dignity.

"You take away a man's dignity… you take away everything. And that's what they took from me, Karina… That's what they took… from me, my father, and even our brothers. They *took* our dignity away from us. Yes, they may have taken us away from our homes and even from our families, but what they took most of all… was our dignity. Now we have nothing left… *I* have nothing left, because they took it all! They took everything, Karina!" He begins to shout. "Everything…Those *evil, evil* people… white devils, they took everything… *everything*… Awwwww!" He screams as he overturns a table. He then picks up a chair and throws it against the wall. Once the chair hits the wall, it shatters into pieces.

"…Emmanuel," Karina then says as she looks at the smashed chair with glazed eyes. "…That was my only chair." Upon saying these words, Emmanuel looks at her with an odd expression. "Now where am I going to sit?" she asks him. "You know, I don't have much in this world these days," she pitifully adds. "All I had… was that chair… and now it's gone Emmanuel… it's gone."

Emmanuel, still staring, begins to laugh.

"Damn it, Karina!" he then says. "I can't stay mad around you!"

"Just trying to lighten the mood," she says as she stretches out her arms for a hug. For a second, Emmanuel stares at Karina's open arms. He then goes over and gives her a hug.

Now in each other's embrace, Karina says to him, "Emmanuel, life isn't fair. In fact, sometimes it can just be downright cruel. No, I do not know what it feels like to be a man, but I do know that every person wants to be loved, valued, and validated… even men. Sometimes people even need to hear an apology so they can feel that their feelings are heard and even received.

"So, Emmanuel," Karina says as she holds his face in the palm of her hands, "I apologize. I apologize for you being taken away from your birth family. I apologize for you being taken away from Ruth, Kevin, and the new family you came to love. I apologize for you being captured, kept in a dungeon, put on a ship, and then forced to work as a slave. I apologize. I apologize for the many upon many of times you were beaten. I apologize for all the times you were talked down to. I apologize for all the people who made you feel less than or even like a disease. I apologize. I apologize for the moment you had to witness seeing your birth father surrender... I apologize. And most of all Emmanuel... *most of all*... I apologize for everyone and/or anyone who stole your dignity away from you... I apologize."

As Karina continues to hold Emmanuel in her embrace, tears begin to well up in his eyes. Quickly breaking away, he faces the other direction, and as he does, he discreetly wipes the tears from his eyes. Karina, going beside him, rests a hand on his shoulder. Emmanuel, now looking at her, shows tears that are now streaming down his face. Emmanuel and Karina then give each other a hug once more, and while doing so, Emmanuel says to her, "Thanks, Sis... thanks for the apology. I needed to hear that."

"You're welcome... I love you, Brother."

"I love you too, Sis... and sorry I broke your chair."

"...Me too. Well, now that you have broken something, you feel better?"

"Actually," he then says as he withdraws from the embrace and looks off to the side, "I do."

"Good," Karina says as she laughs a little.

Later that night, after Emmanuel has left, Karina lies asleep in her bed, and as she sleeps, she tosses and turns while saying, "No, no, don't do it, *no*... Emmanuel!" She then sits up and shouts.

"Bad dream?" she hears Abaven suddenly say. Looking, Karina sees Abaven standing by the door.

"Yes," she tells him. "My brother Emmanuel is filled with such hate and anger, and I dreamed that his hate and anger destroyed him. Oh, Abaven," she then gets out of bed and goes over to him, "Please don't let it be so. Please do something."

"I myself have no power unless it is given to me by God, and even God himself is a God of free will. He doesn't make someone do something that they don't want to do."

"Well, can I continue to talk to him?"

"You should... but understand this: Whether or not he takes heed to your words, Karina is his decision and his decision alone."

Upon hearing Abaven's words, Karina looks to the floor to ponder the thought.

Chapter 39

T HE NEXT MORNING, AS KARINA FINISHES WRAPPING A turban on her head, a knock is heard at the front door. Going toward the door and opening it, she sees Emmanuel standing there. "Good morning, Sis," he says with a smile.

"God Almighty, Emmanuel. What is that on your face?"

"What?" Emmanuel questions as he paranoidly feels his face.

"It's a smile," Karina says as she laughs a little. "A smile! And it sure is nice to see you wearing one."

"Why, thank you."

"So, how did you sleep?"

"Unfortunately, not well, because I was still very angry."

"Oh, Emmanuel."

"But don't worry, Sis. I made good use of my anger."

"Huh, oh... What did you do?"

"I did this." Still standing outside, Emmanuel reaches to the side and pulls a wooden chair into view. "For you, Sis," he then says with a big smile on his face as he holds the chair in his hand. "I made it myself."

"A chair!" Karina says with glee. "You made me a new chair!"

"I did... You like it?"

"I love it... Thank you," she says as she places the chair inside.

Just then, Karina and Emmanuel hear the bell being rung.

"Well," Emmanuel then says, "Let's get to the field so we can begin our labor for the day."

"Yes."

Karina and Emmanuel begin walking towards the field, and as they do, Karina looks down at the ground. "Yeah, I really felt bad about destroying your chair, Sis. Even though I was angry, I shouldn't have... Karina... Sis?" He then says when he sees her looking down, "What's on your mind?"

"You said something last night that I still can't get out of my mind."

"Well, I said a lot of things, so was there one thing particular?"

"White devils."

"Oh, that… Well, Karina… they are."

"They are, are they?"

"Yes."

"Well, tell me, Emmanuel. Mother and Father was white… Was they white devils too?"

"Of course, not Karina, Mother and Father wasn't white devils."

"And why wasn't they?"

"Because."

"Because?"

"Because they were different."

"And why were they different?"

"Because they were, Karina. Because they chose to be, I guess."

"Exactly… because they chose to be. Emmanuel, the choices that people make, whether bad or good, they make them because of what's inside their heart, not because of the color of their skin. And the choices that people do even make, they make because they feel it's the only way they can survive."

As Karina and Emmanuel approach the back porch of Ehmerney's house, Ehmerney overhears their conversation. The words that Karina has spoken begin echoing throughout his mind. "The choices that people make, whether bad or good, they make it because of what's inside their heart, not because of the color of their skin." As he continues to dwell on her words, Ehmerney's mind flashes back to an earlier time on the plantation when he was just eighteen years of age.

While standing on the front porch, he sees his father standing there and looking at another older Caucasian man who's looking over a male slave.

"Good," says the older Caucasian to Ehmerney's father. "Very good… I'll take him. How much?"

"Three thousand, Fredrick."

"Three thousand? Wait," Fredrick then says as he begins laughing, "You're messing with me, aren't you, Johnathan? You always were a trickster."

"I'm not joking… $3,000!"

"Three thousand!? Are you kidding me? Johnathan, you're asking price for this slave is twice than what you paid for him, plus you had him for nearly fifteen years, so he definitely has some work put into him."

"Yes, but the price is still the same... Do you want him, yes or no?"

"Johnathan, you and I have been friends for over thirty years, and I'm struggling just like you... You can't help me out and lower the cost?"

"No."

"Well, can I at least pay you half now and half later?"

"No. I need all the money now!"

"Johnathan, I really need the extra help, but it's going to take all I have just to purchase this one slave. There's no way you can help me out, and what about that favor I did for you last summer?"

"I thank you, but unfortunately, I can't lower the cost."

Upon hearing his answer, Fredrick looks to the ground and sighs. "Fine, Johnathan," he then looks at him and angrily says, "Fine!" He then hastily takes the money out of his pocket and prepares to give it to him. However, just before placing the money in his hands, he says to him, "Just so we are clear... *this*... changes everything between you and I."

"I understand," Johnathan coldly responds.

He then harshly places the money into Johnathan's hands. "Put the slave into the wagon!" he then heatedly tells a younger man who happens to be with him. As he makes his way toward the driver's seat, he crossly looks at Johnathan one last time. Now in the wagon, he hastily begins driving away.

Once Fredrick has left, Johnathan turns and faces Ehmerney. "What?" he says, irritated, when he sees Ehmerney staring at him.

"I didn't say anything, Father," Ehmerney tells him.

"No, you didn't, but you're standing there and looking at me with those judgmental eyes of yours. You especially should know how hard things have been for us lately, and sometimes you have to do what you have to do to survive."

"Yes, Father," Ehmerney says timidly.

For a second, he stares meanly at his son. "Oh, I don't expect you to understand," he then says, "You're too young... You're too young to understand anything," he says. As he waves his hands towards him in disgust, Johnathan goes inside the house, leaving Ehmerney on the porch alone, and as he stands there, he looks off the porch to ponder his father's words.

A harsh wind causes Ehmerney's flashback to come to an end. Looking up toward the sky, he sees that the fierce wind is being complemented by growing dark clouds.

"Father!" Ehmerney then hears his son shout. Looking, Ehmerney sees his son Johnathan standing at the back doorway. "There's a really bad storm coming... We must get inside and to the basement to take cover!"

Heeding his son's warning, Ehmerney begins heading inside. "Richard, come," his wife frantically tells him as she makes her way toward the basement door.

For a moment, Ehmerney stands there and gazes at her, and as he does, Karina's words come to mind. "The choices that people make, whether bad or good, they make because of what's inside their heart, not because of the color of their skin."

"I have to make sure the slaves get shelter," Ehmerney then says as he heads toward the front porch.

"Richard, no, come back!" Martha screams.

"Father!"

However, Ehmerney continues walking. Now on the front porch, he screams, "Jason!"

"Yes, Master!"

"There's a really bad storm coming... Ring the bell and tell all the slaves to head back to their cabins to take cover!"

"Yes, Master!"

While dark clouds become more visible and the wind begins to blow fiercely, a bell is heard ringing. As the bell continues to ring, Freddy runs up to Karina. Screaming in a high-pitched sound, he frantically jumps up and down while pointing at the sky.

"Yes, Jason, I know," says Karina as she watches Freddy display such trepidation. "There's a storm coming. I know."

"Karina, Master wants us to take cover," Sarah suddenly says as she and Lisa approach her.

"Okay, but first let me go get my..."

"Brother?" Emmanuel says as Karina turns and sees him standing there. "Let's head for cover."

"Yes, we can stay in my cabin," says Sarah.

"Well, lead the way," Emmanuel tells her.

The five of them begin making their way toward Sarah's cabin. However, just before entering...

Chapter 40

RAIN BEGINS TO POUR. THEY MANAGE TO GET IN-
side, but due to the intensity of the wind, Sarah struggles
to close the door. Freddy and Emmanuel, noticing her
effort, help push the door closed. Once the door is closed, Emmanuel looks
at everyone and asks, "Is everyone okay?"

"We're okay," says Karina.

"Well, we are now," Lisa adds.

"God Almighty, that storm is something else," says Karina.

"Sure is," says Sarah.

Just then, they hear a loud crashing sound. "Oooooo," Freddy moans
in fear as he moves away from the door.

"Was that thundering?" Lisa asks.

"No, it sounded like something fell," says Emmanuel. "Something *has*
fallen," he adds as he looks out the window... *look!*"

"Karina, Sarah, and Lisa, looking out the window, see that a large pine
tree has fallen on Ehmerney's house, destroying the roof of the porch while
the rest of the house remains intact.

"God Almighty," says Karina as she watches in horror. "I pray no one
has gotten hurt."

"I pray they *have*," says Emmanuel. "Then we'll all be free!"

"Emmanuel," says Karina as she sadly looks at him.

"So, is that your name... Emmanuel," Freddy asks.

"Yes, that's my name... not no dang gone Harry."

"Hey, wait a minute," says Sarah. "I heard about you... You're that
new slave that's been giving Master and Jason so much trouble?"

"Is that what you heard?" Emmanuel asks.

"Yes," Sarah, Freddy, and Lisa simultaneously say.

"Well, good," Emmanuel replies with a smile.

"Oh, Emmanuel," Karina then says as she shakes her head and rolls
her eyes.

"But never mind what you heard already… I'm just getting started."

"Emmanuel, please! Stop talking like that! Don't let your hate and anger control you."

"And why in the hell should I not?"

"Because last night I dreamed that…"

"That what?" he asks in expectation.

"Nothing," Karina then says when she notices Sarah, Lisa, and Freddy staring at her. "I'll tell you later."

"Well, that was a quick storm," says Sarah as she goes back toward the window. "It's over already."

"I wonder if Master wants us to go back to the field," says Lisa. At that moment, they hear the bell being rung.

"Does *that* answer your question?" Karina tells her

As the five of them make their way out of the cabin, they see a soggy ground with fallen tree branches everywhere.

"Well, let's head back towards the field," says Sarah.

They begin to walk when suddenly Karina discreetly calls, "Emmanuel?"

"What?" he answers as he turns to look at her.

"Come here," she says as she motions.

"What?" he says as he draws close. "What is it?"

"I wanted to talk to you about some of the things you said while we were inside."

"Oh, Karina. I was just joking… Honestly, you take things way too seriously."

"Well, maybe a little while ago you were joking, but you weren't joking last night when you screamed and hollered and threw my chair against the wall."

"Karina," he says, annoyed, "for the umpteenth time, I'm sorry about the chair."

"Yes, I know, but what about all the trouble you had with Jason… and how about you almost killing Master?"

"What about it?"

"Don't you think that's a problem?"

"For them, yeah," he says as he laughs a little. "But not for me."

"But it can be a problem for you, Emmanuel."

"I doubt it. I can handle myself, Sis. I did it several times before with the other masters. At most, they'll just get tired of me and send me away."

"No Emmanuel... not this time."

"Yeah, this time too! Because they can't handle me, Sis... Nobody can."

He begins arrogantly walking away when Karina suddenly shouts, "Emmanuel, for the love of God, will you listen to me? I'm trying to tell you something!"

"Okay, Sis, calm down," he responds as he draws back closer to her and grabs a hand. "What are you trying to tell me?"

Inhaling then exhaling, Karina says, "Last night, I had a dream about you. A bad dream. I dreamed that you were in a situation here on this plantation, and you were filled with hate and anger. And because of that, you were destroyed."

"Oh, that was just a bad dream, Karina," Emmanuel tells her as he hugs her. "Just a bad, bad dream. I'll be fine."

"You won't be fine if you don't hurry up and get back to the field," they suddenly hear Jason say.

Upon hearing Jason's words, Emmanuel opens his mouth to say something smart, but Karina quickly grabs his hand and interjects, "Okay, Mr. Jason... We're on our way."

After Jason has walked away, Emmanuel looks at Karina and says, "Why didn't you let me curse him out?"

"Because you're in enough trouble as it is. Come on... let's get to the field." Once near the field, Karina and Emmanuel witness the large pine tree that has fallen on Master Ehmerney's house. "God Almighty," says Karina as she stares in awe.

"Hopefully, there are some casualties," says Emmanuel as he stares at the disastrous sight as well.

"Harry!" Ehmerney then calls from the unaffected side of the porch.

"Oh darn," Emmanuel then says once seeing him. "He's still alive." Emmanuel looks at him and answers with a fake smile, "Yes, Master."

"Go get an axe and help chop up this tree so they can get it off my porch roof."

"Yes, Master!" Emmanuel says, still with an artificial smile.

"I gotta go." Emmanuel then looks at Karina seriously and says, "Catch up to you later, Sis." After kissing her on the cheek, he walks away.

Karina, still in place, sees that the now fallen tree has given sight to a white house that's sitting at the top of a mountain. As her eyes remain fixated on the house, she stares oddly.

"Stop lollygagging and get to work." Jason then tells her as he walks up behind her.

"Yes, Mr. Jason," she looks at him and says, as she begins heading back toward the field, she discreetly looks at the house one more time.

Chapter 41

THAT EVENING, KARINA SITS OUTSIDE HER CABIN AND UN-
derneath a tree. Standing to her feet, she makes her way to Ehmerney's house and stops where the tree has fallen. Standing there, she
looks at the white house that sits at the top of the hill. stares at the white
house that's on top of the mountain. As she continues to stare, she hears a
male voice from behind. "You can't seem to stop staring at that house, can
you?"

Turning toward the voice, she sees Donkor standing there.

"No, Papa, I can't. It feels as though the house is calling me."

"What if I told you it was… What if I told you God wanted you to go
there?"

"To go there? Oh, no, I couldn't possibly do that. I could get in really
big trouble if I do that."

"Abena, God wants to take your faith to a whole new level by chal-
lenging you to go there."

"I don't think I can. I'm not brave enough."

"You are," Donkor tells her as he draws close. "You are brave enough.
After all, you are from the African tribe *Gurunsi*."

Once Donkor has vanished into thin air, Karina returns to her cabin,
and as she sits underneath the tree outside her cabin once more, her mind
drifts back to a time in Africa when she was nine years of age. While sitting
on the lake's shore, Karina watches as her brothers Emmanuel, Joshua,
Daniel, and Victor get baptized. Suddenly, her father, Kevin, sits beside her.
"It's almost your turn… Are you ready?"

"No," Karina says as she shakes her head. "I'm not going."

"How come?"

"I'm afraid of the water."

"I understand why you are afraid. I understand… You probably don't
even remember this, but the day your mother and I found you, we found
you in the water, drowning, and even though we rescued you, still, you

always had this fear of water since then. So, if you don't want to get in the water and get baptized, your mother and I will be okay with that."

"You will!?" Karina says with a surprised look on her face.

"Yes… we will… but will *you* be okay with that? You see, as long as you remain fearful of that water… then the water will always have power over you… Can you live with that?"

"I do not want to live with that, Father… but I'm afraid."

"It's okay to be afraid. I get afraid too sometimes."

"You do?"

"I do. But I choose to be courageous because I realize that courage only becomes courage in the face of fear. Think about that." Kevin then gets up and walks away. Karina, still seated, ponders Kevin's words. She then stands to her feet and slowly begins making her way toward the lake. With the water now touching the tip of her toes, she looks back at Kevin. Standing beside him is Ruth, who's holding a two-year old Bryan on her hip. As he sees Karina looking at him, he gives her a wink and then a smile. Karina, smiling as well, begins slowly making her way further into the water. With the water now waist high, she feels as though her heart is about to pop out of her chest, but her nervousness is met with the comfort of an African priest who reaches out and takes hold of her arm.

"It's okay," the priest reassures her. "It's okay… I got you. You take one step, and God will take two. Are you ready?"

"I am."

After facing her forward, he then says, "Karina… in the name of the Father, the Son and the Holy Spirit, I baptized you."

Taking a deep breath then holding it, Karina gets baptized.

"Karina," she suddenly hears Emmanuel call as her flashback comes to an end.

"Yes, Emmanuel," she answers as she stands to her feet."

"I see you over here sitting underneath the tree… Is everything okay?" he asks as he approaches her.

"I'm fine. Just thinking about that white house that I saw at the top of the hill this morning… Did you see it too?"

"Yes, I happened to see it. What about it?"

"God wants me to go there… He wants *us* to go there, Emmanuel," she tells him. "I don't know what will happen if we do, but we have to take that step of faith. If we take one step… then God will take two."

"Okay, Sis… okay, I receive that… So, when do we leave?"

"Let's leave tomorrow night. Right now, everything is still wet and slippery from the storm."

"Tomorrow night it is."

"But we must not allow for anyone or anything to distract us. I really want us to go together, Emmanuel, so promise me... promise me. Promise you will keep your heart and mind centered. Promise!"

"I promise," he says with a light laugh.

"I love you, Emmanuel," Karina then says as she gives him a hug.

"I love you too, Sis," Emmanuel says as he embraces her in return.

"See you tomorrow," says Karina.

"Yes... tomorrow."

As Karina goes into her cabin, Emmanuel begins walking away. Once at his cabin door, he begins to go inside but stops and reminisces on Karina's words. "We must not allow for anyone or anything to distract us," he recalls her saying.

"Distract," he then says, "Why does that word seem so familiar?" Letting out a sigh, he goes to a nearby log and sits down, and while staring at the moon, he begins thinking back to the time when he first met his father, Kevin.

While a nine-year-old Emmanuel hides in the bush with two of his younger brothers, he sees the youngest brother standing outside of the bush. "Why are you out there?" he asks him in the Gur language

"I wanna see wagon," the youngest brother replies in the Gur language as well.

"No," Emmanuel tells him, "Get back in here! We must not allow for any outside noise to distract us from keeping safe... so come on... get back in here!"

Upon hearing his oldest brother's demand, the youngest brother returns to hiding in the bush. However, after a few seconds of returning, footsteps are heard from outside. "Someone is coming!" one of the brothers says as they hear the footsteps getting closer.

"See what you've done," Emmanuel says, looking at his youngest brother.

Once the footsteps reach the bush, they stop. Suddenly, a hand moves back the branches and peaking inside is a Caucasian man with blonde hair and blue eyes. "Hi," the man then says, "My name is Kevin. I'm here to help you." Emmanuel and his brothers, looking with fear, give no reply. "Let me help you," he adds. He then extends a hand inside.

However, just before touching any of them, Emmanuel jumps up and out of the bush. Tackling Kevin to the ground, he begins violently pounding on his neck, face, and chest.

"No! No," Kevin screams as he tries to block his hits. "I want to help you, please... Let me help you."

"Let me help you," Emmanuel then remembers Kevin saying to him years later while they both sit in front of a fireplace in Africa. "I want to help you. Please. Let me help you. But first, answer this... Do you control your anger, or does your anger control you?"

As the flashback comes to an end, Kevin's words echo throughout Emmanuel's mind... "Do you control your anger or does your anger control you?"

Sighing, Emmanuel looks to the ground to ponder his words.

The next day, as the bell rings, Karina and Emmanuel head toward the field. "So, how did you sleep last night, Emmanuel?"

"I slept well this time."

"Good, because we gonna need our strength for our journey to..." Karina stops talking when she and Emmanuel draw close to the field and see a crowd of slaves surrounding a tree, and while standing there, whispers and whimpering cries are heard in the crowd. "What on Earth is all of this? Huh... God Almighty." Karina then gasps when she looks and sees a male slave hanging from a tree. "Sarah," Karina then asks when she sees her standing nearby, "what happened?"

"He tried to run away during the storm, but they caught him, and he was lynched.

As Karina continues to look at the hanging man, Ehmerney comes walking out on to the back porch. "That's what will happen to a slave if he tries to run away," he says to the crowd.

Upon hearing Ehmerney's words, Emmanuel leans over and whispers to Karina, "You still wanna take that journey, Sis?"

With a glazed look in her eyes, Karina looks at him and says....

Purpose Me

Me

Choosing to be Courageous

Volume 4

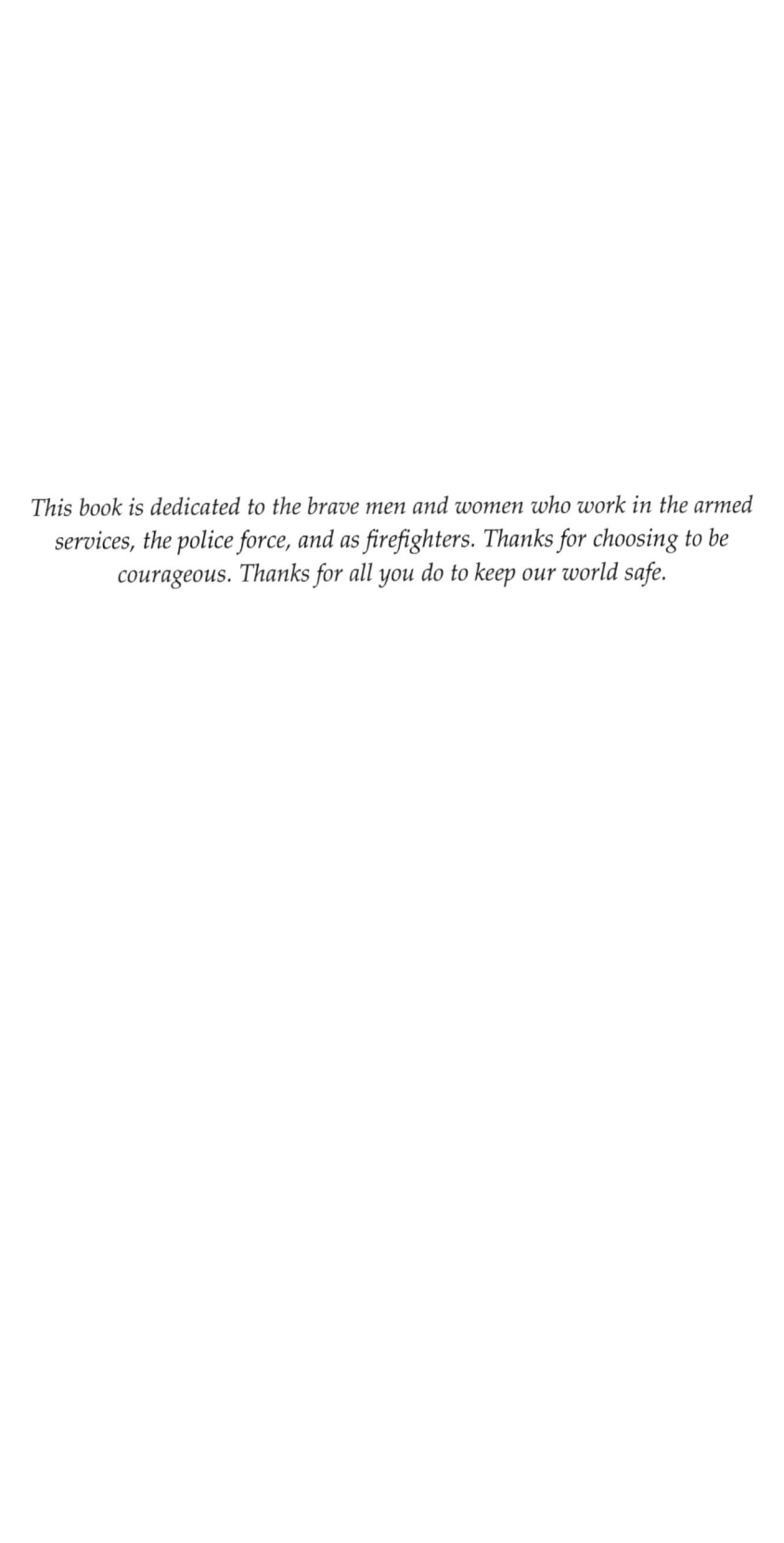

This book is dedicated to the brave men and women who work in the armed services, the police force, and as firefighters. Thanks for choosing to be courageous. Thanks for all you do to keep our world safe.

Chapter 1

E ARLY IN THE MORNING, AS THE BELL RINGS, KARINA AND Emmanuel head toward the field. "So, how did you sleep last night, Emmanuel?"

"I slept well this time."

"Good, because we gonna need our strength for our journey to…" Karina stops talking when she and Emmanuel draw close to the field and see a crowd of slaves surrounding a tree, and while standing there, whispers and whimpering cries are heard in the crowd. "What on Earth is all of this? Huh… God Almighty." Karina then gasps when she looks and sees a male slave hanging from a tree. "Sarah," Karina asks when she sees her standing nearby, "what happened?"

"He tried to run away during the storm, but they caught him, and he was lynched."

As Karina continues to look at the man hanging from the tree, Ehmerney comes walking out on the back porch. "That's what will happened to a slave if he tries to run away," he says to Karina and the slaves.

Upon hearing Ehmerney's words, Emmanuel whispers in Karina's ear, "You still wanna take that journey, Sis?"

Pausing for a moment, Karina looks at him and confidently says, "Yes… I'm still gonna take the journey."

"Wow, you're brave. How did you become so courageous?"

"I'm not, Emmanuel, not courageous at all. I'm actually terrified… But father once told me that courage only becomes courage in the face of fear."

"Father was a very wise man," says Emmanuel as he kisses her on the temple.

"Alright, everyone," Ehmerney then says, "That's enough gazing and crying, now get to work."

"Well, let me finish getting this tree off of Ehmerney's roof," Emmanuel then tells her.

"Okay, but please, Emmanuel, stay out of trouble today… *please!*"

"I will, Sis, because *I* control my anger, my anger doesn't control me… at least that's what father told me."

"Amen," Karina replies with a smile.

"Well, another day in the field," suddenly says Sarah as she, Freddy, and Lisa approach her.

"Yeah, let's grab our buckets," says Karina.

"Not so fast," then says Jason. "Master wants the four of you to go into the woods, to the place where they normally bury the slaves. Find a spot, and clear it off so when the men dig the ditch for the hanging body, they won't have any problems."

"Yes, Mr. Jason," Karina and the rest of them say.

As Ehmerney stands on the back porch, he looks at the dead slave's body that's still hanging from the tree, and as he continues to stare, his wife joins him on the porch.

"Another slave lynched?" she asks while watching.

"Another slave Lynched," he responds with a sigh.

"I thought you didn't like lynching slaves."

"I don't. That's why I had the four male slaves do it. We can't have slaves running away, Martha. We just can't. We need to make that very clear to the other slaves. If not, more of them will try to run away, and then I'll be the laughing stock of South Carolina and not to mention an embarrassment to my family."

As Ehmerney continues watching the men cutting the dead slave down from the tree, he begins to reminisce on an earlier moment he experienced on the plantation, when he was just eighteen years of age. Ehmerney remembers standing in the barn with a dark-skinned African girl, and as they hold each other close, she asks him…

"So, how do you feel about all of this: the plantation, people working here as slaves… How do you feel about it?"

"I don't like it," he tells her. "I don't like it at all. Today, for the first time, I watched my father and a couple of other men lynch a slave. It was so upsetting to see. I still can't get over the look that slave had in his eyes when he was being hanged. I really don't like any of this. None of the things that happen here on the plantation feel right to me."

"Well, if you feel something in your heart that's not right, maybe it's God's way of trying to tell you something."

"So, what am I supposed to do, huh?" he hastily says as he withdraws from the embrace. "Go against my very own father, go against everything he taught me and even everything he expects of me? I'm not courageous enough to do that. Everything that my father is doing has been done in my family for generations. I can't change that."

"So, what will you do then, Richard... spend the rest of your life living a lie?"

"To please my father... yes."

"So, what about us, Richard? What about the feelings you have for me... Is that a lie?

"Oh, no, my love," he says as he draws back close to her. "My feelings for you are true; I do love you, even if we have to meet in pri—"

Suddenly, the barn door opens, and in comes Ehmerney's father. As he stands there with his arms folded, he stands with an angry look on his face.

"Richard, in the house now!" he tells him, "*Now!*" he then shouts

Upon hearing his father's demand, Ehmerney quickly leaves the barn.

As the flashback comes to an end, Ehmerney sighs as he watches the four African men begin taking the dead body down from the tree.

As Karina, Lisa, Freddy, and Sarah approach the woods, Jason walks behind them. "Alright, we gonna find a spot for that dead slave then clear it off really wel..." but he stops talking when he looks and sees Emmanuel standing by a woodpile, sharpening an axe. "You guys go ahead," Jason then tells him. "And make sure you clean off that spot really good, too." Jason begins making his way over to the woodpile where Emmanuel is. Once there, he stands behind him and watches him with a smirk on his face.

"What?" Emmanuel asks Jason when he stops and looks at him.

"Nothing," Jason replies.

Emmanuel resumes chopping.

"What?" Emmanuel stops, looks at him, and asks once more.

"Nothing, man."

"I really don't have time for your nonsense today, Jason."

"What are you talking about, man? I'm not doing anything, I'm just standing here."

"Just standing there, huh?"

"Yeah."

"Yeah, okay."

He begins chopping some wood when suddenly Jason says, "I hate to break this to you... but you swing that axe like a girl."

Dropping the axe, Emmanuel looks at him and says, "What, is your problem *man*... Why you acting like this? What... what happened?

Somebody picked on you when you were a child or something, so now you're mad."

"Hey, you leave my childhood out of this," Jason says as he draws close to him with tears in his eyes. "Just like I'll leave your sister out of this," he then adds as he walks away a little.

"You didn't learn anything from that kick?" Emmanuel then asks.

"You didn't learn anything from that beating?" Jason replies.

"You know what, Jason... I'm not dealing with you today... I'm not!"

"Why not?" Jason then asks as he sees Emmanuel return to chopping wood. "What happened since we last spoke. What? You decided to give your sister your balls for safekeeping."

"You son of a...."

"Son of a what?"

"Nope. Nope," Emmanuel then says. "I'm not going to let you get to me this time. No. I'm just going to ignore you and finish chopping this wood."

"Well, that's good, man. You go ahead and ignore me. Harry... Hateful Harry, and I hope you be ignoring me tonight when I'll be making sweet love to your sister."

Upon hearing Jason's words, Emmanuel stops and looks at him with hate in his eyes.

In the woods, after Karina, Lisa, Sara, and Freddy found a spot for the dead slave to be buried, they begin clearing it. Stopping, Karina looks around to see who might be present besides her and her friends.

"What?" Sarah asks as she looks at Karina with an odd expression. "Why are you looking around?"

"There's something I need to tell you guys, and I just wanna make sure Jason, Master, or anyone else is not around to hear it."

"Hear what?" Freddy asks

Inhaling then exhaling, Karina looks at them and says, "I'm leaving the plantation tonight!"

"Karina, you've been sold to another Master?" Lisa asks.

"No! Emmanuel and I are running away."

"What?" they all answer with a surprise look on their faces.

"Tonight, after it gets really, really dark."

"Are you crazy?" says Freddy, "You didn't see what just happened to that other slave? We're even here clearing off his burial plot."

"Freddy is right," says Sarah. "You could get caught and lynched, too. Then we'll be here clearing off a spot for *you*. Besides, why you wanna leave us, Karina? I thought we were your friends."

"You are my friends... my very dear friends... which is why I want you to come with me."

"Oh no," says Sarah, "I'm not going anywhere... I'm staying right here. I'm staying where it's comfortable and not to mention safe. A place where no one gets hurt or even offended... especially me. This place is a nice place to be in Karina... very nice."

"Nice? Sarah, we're slaves here!" says Karina.

"Maybe we are, but we have a place to lay our heads, and we get food that we never have to buy. It's not a great life, Karina, but it's a good one. Honestly, Karina, you must learn how to be grateful for what you have."

"Grateful? For this? We live in cabins that are extremely hot in the summer and terribly cold in the winter. The so-called beds... consist of a wooden surface, not a mattress, and the food they give us is leftovers from their own meals. Oh yeah," Karina says as she throws her arms up in the air in frustration, "I definitely should be grateful for this. I'm living the life. What more should I possibly want?"

"Well, I'll go with you, Karina," says Lisa.

"You will?"

"Yes, I will. Just tell me what we need to do."

"Well, after midnight we're gonna leave here then climb the mountain and after that we should..."

"Wait... wait, did you just say climb a mountain?"

"Yes, I did."

"Never mind, I'm not going. That's too much work."

"But Lisa... we're not just climbing a mountain; we're climbing toward our freedom."

"I'd rather stay a slave."

"What's the matter with all of you? Don't you see, you're living a life you don't have to. You don't have to be Settle Sarah, Lazy Lisa, or Fearful Freddy. You don't have to be those people that Jason says you are. Jason even gave me a name, calling me Defeated Denise. But I'm no Defeated Denise. I'm Karina... and I choose to be courageous. So, what do you say? Do you wanna leave here and go for something better... Sarah?"

"I'm fine just where I'm at."

"Freddy?"

"No, Karina. I'm too scared."

"Lisa," Karina then asks but doesn't see her anywhere. "Li—" she asks once more as she begins looking around but stops when she sees that Lisa is sitting down on a nearby log, not doing anything. "Never mind," Karina then says as she shakes her head and rolls her eyes.

Suddenly, Karina and the three of them hear a loud crash.

"What was that?" Freddy fearfully asks.

"I don't know," Karina replies as she stands to her feet, "Look!" she then shouts as she points toward the forest opening, "There's people running toward something!"

"Well, what on Earth could they be running towards?" says Sarah as she and the others stand to their feet.

"Well, there's only one way to find out." Says Karina.

As they come out of the woods, they see hundreds of slaves surrounding the woodpile while chanting, "Get him! Get him!"

"What's going on there?" Freddy asks as he and the others quizzically stare.

"I don't know; it looks like a fight," says Sarah. "Honestly, where's Jason when you need him?"

"Last I saw, he left us and headed there," says Lisa.

"Emmanuel went there," Karina then says to herself as she looks off to the side. "Emmanuel," she then shouts as she begins running towards the scene. There, she maneuvers her way through the crowd to get an up-close view of what is going on. "God Almighty," she then shouts when she sees...

Chapter 2

EMMANUEL, STANDING BEHIND JASON, WHILE HE has both arms wrapped tightly around his neck.

"Get him! Get him!" the crowd continues to chant, encouraging Emmanuel.

"Man, what are you doing?" an African man from the crowd then shouts. "Squeeze his neck harder!" he tells Emmanuel.

"Emmanuel," Karina then shouts, "what in the world is going on here?"

"I'm tired of him, Karina. I'm tired of him always messing with me... I'll snap his neck... I swear to God I will."

"No, Emmanuel," Karina says with tears in her eyes. "No... You're better than that."

"Am I? I'm hateful Harry, remember? At least that's what they call me: Hateful Harry."

"No, Emmanuel, you're not Hateful Harry, or at least you don't have to be. Come on, Emmanuel," Karina says as she stretches out her arms toward him. "Come on and let's get out of here. Come on."

Upon hearing her words, Emmanuel stares at her with tears in his eyes.

"Come on!" Karina says once more.

Emmanuel then harshly throws Jason to the side. He then draws close to Karina. Once there, he gives her a hug.

Withdrawing from the embrace, Karina asks, "Are you okay?"

"No," Jason answers instead as he stumbles to his feet.

Upon hearing Jason's response, Karina and Emmanuel glance at him for a second. "Are *you*?" Karina then looks at Emmanuel and asks again as she disregards Jason's answer.

"Yes," Emmanuel answers as she shakes his head.

"After tonight, we won't have to deal with this anymore," Karina whispers to Emmanuel as they both begin walking away.

"Yes, tomorrow will bring a new day," Emmanuel replies.

Just then, Ehmerney comes onto the scene. "What's going on here?"

"It's Harry again, Master," says Jason. "And this time he tried to kill me."

"Harry! You causing trouble again?"

"I'm not causing trouble. He started with me!"

"I find that very hard to believe. You've been trouble ever since you got here. No wonder why those men gave you to me for free. You're nothing but drama."

"I'm not," Emmanuel tells him. "I was just chopping wood when Ja—"

But Karina interrupts. "Emmanuel," she whispers, "don't worry about explaining yourself. Let's just get out of here. *Please.*"

As Emmanuel and Karina begin walking away, Ehmerney says, "My wife was right. You're no good for anything. All you are… is just one crazy slave."

"Do you hear him, Karina?" Emmanuel asks with teary eyes. "Do you hear him talking to me like that?"

"Yes, Emmanuel," Karina says as she tries to hurry him along. "I hear him… But just ignore him."

"Who does he think he's talking to like that?"

"I know, but just come on… Don't look back!"

But Emmanuel does look back.

"Who do you think you're talking to like that?" he then shouts to Ehmerney.

"I'm your master; that's who I am."

"Well, you're no master of me, you no good son of a—"

"Emmanuel!" Karina interjects, "just come on."

"Jonathan," Ehmerney then says to his son, who's standing nearby, "bring me my whip!"

"Oh, now you gonna whip me… You gonna *whip* me… Well, you won't get a chance to whip me this time, 'cause I'll kill you. You hear me? I'll kill you… white devil… I'll kill you! I'll kill you before I let you whip me again."

"I would like to see you try."

Karina, now seeing the hate in Emmanuel's eyes, begins to say, "No… no… no Emmanuel, don't do it. No, Emmanuel!"

"Awwww," he then screams as he charges toward Ehmerney. Emmanuel, now in front of him, picks Ehmerney up by the neck, then pins him to a nearby tree.

"Urrrr," Ehmerney sounds as he tries to get Emmanuel's hands off his neck. "Johnathan," he then manages to say, "get the gun... get the—" But his words are cut short due to the intensity of Emmanuel's hands on his neck. Ehmerney then manages to press his fingers into Emmanuel's eyes.

"Awww," Emmanuel screams as he releases his grip, then looks away to aid his eyes.

Ehmerney then takes off running, with Emmanuel seeing then chasing after him. He nearly reaches Ehmerney when suddenly, a gunshot rings out from behind...

"Huh?" Emmanuel stops and gasps as he feels a sharp pain in the center of his back. The pain then transfers to his chest. Looking down... Emmanuel sees blood gushing out of a small bullet hole that's in the center of his chest.

He then faces Karina, who's now looking at him while crying profusely. "Emmanuel," she then says with a whimpering cry. His eyes roll to the back of his head, then... he falls to the ground... face first. Karina, going over, kneels down beside him. She then gently faces him toward her. Emmanuel's eyes, still open, stare at her, and as they do, he grabs tightly onto Karina's shirt. With his breathing now shallow, Karina says to him, "Why didn't you listen to me... Why didn't you just walk away?"

Leaning his head toward Karina's bosom, Emmanuel closes his eyes... and dies.

Chapter 3

HOURS LATER, IN A WOODED AREA, KARINA SITS IN FRONT of a freshly buried grave. Looking at the other slave graves around her, she notices they are unmarked. "No," she then says while looking back at the spot where Emmanuel is now buried. "No! You will not have an unmarked grave. You may have been cheated in life, but you will *not* be cheated in death." Karina then sees a medium-sized gray stone with a sharp edge to the right of her. She slices a finger on the stone's sharp edge, and it begins to bleed heavily. With the blood from her finger, she writes "Emmanuel" on the stone. She then places the stone at the head of his burial plot. As she gazes at the stone and his plot with a very despondent look on her face, she hears echoing in her mind, "Defeated, defeated, defeated..."

"Denise," Ehmerney then calls as he approaches her from behind but stops from a few feet away.

"Yes, Master," Karina answers while still staring, "You called my name?"

"I did. You been here long enough; now get back to the field."

"Yes, Master."

Karina stands and faces him, and for a moment, she stares at him with a hateful look in her eyes. She then begins making her way to the field.

Once Karina has walked away, Ehmerney goes to the family cemetery that's located near the plantation. There he kneels down in front of a tombstone that reads, "Johnathan Ehmerney 1747–1798."

"I had a slave killed today," Ehmerney says while staring at the tombstone, "And actually, there's a part of me that feels rather bad. Hmm... if you were still here and heard me talking like this, I could imagine what you probably would say."

As Ehmerney continues to stare, he thinks back to an earlier time on the plantation, when he was eighteen years old. As he stands in the living room of his home, he sadly looks to the floor, and as he does, his father circles him with an angry look on his face, "A female slave," he then tells him while circling. "You were romancing a female slave? That's disgusting! You are sad... pathetic... and I'm ashamed to call you my son!" Hearing those words causes Ehmerney to look at his father with wide eyes. His father, now standing in front of him, angrily adds while pointing a finger in his face, "You will take your rightful place in this family and help conduct this plantation like you are supposed to... You hear me?"

"Yes," Ehmerney says with now teary eyes. "Yes, Father."

Ehmerney's father then leaves the room, and after doing so, Ehmerney's mother, who happens to be in the room, comes to his side.

"Oh, Richard, give no thought toward your father and his cruel words."

"No, Mother," Ehmerney then says, "he's right. He should be ashamed of me; I have been embarrassment to him and to this entire family. But one day, I will change that... One day, when the plantation is passed down to me, I will make him proud. I will be the type of slave master he wants me to be."

As the flashback comes to an end, Ehmerney hears someone talking. Standing and turning toward the sound, he sees two male slaves in the cotton field talking to each other. Going over toward them, he shouts, "Stop that gibber-gabber and get back to work... git!" Upon hearing his words, the two male slaves quickly part ways. Ehmerney then goes and sits on the front porch. There, he begins smoking his cigar and as he does so, his eyes lay hold of Karina, who's in the field picking cotton and looking gloomy. As he stares, the words of the female slave that he loved echo in his mind: "If you feel something in your heart that's not right, maybe it's God's way of trying to tell you something."

Quickly looking away, he looks at the floor of the porch. "I want to make you proud," Ehmerney then says out loud as he continues staring downward. "I want *you* to be proud of me, Father."

Looking back up, he sits back in his chair and resumes smoking his cigar.

That night, as Karina sits outside her cabin, she sits with her back leaning up against a pine tree. Tears pour profusely from her eyes as she thinks on what has transpired during the day.

"Abena," she then hears a male voice call.

"Papa," she answers, "Is that you?"

"Yes... it is I," Donkor tells her as he walks from behind a nearby tree. "It's time Abena... It's time to leave this place."

"After everything that has happened today, I don't think I can. Emmanuel was supposed to go with me, but now he's dead. I asked my friends to go, but they said no. So now, it is just me. Just me, and I'm not courageous enough to take this journey alone."

"You are, Abena," Ozigbodi tells her as she suddenly appears. "You are Gurunsi."

"Gurunsi? I don't even know who I am anymore, let alone being Gurunsi."

"You don't remember who you are?" Ozigbodi tells her. "Then let me remind you of who you are... You are the type of person who has always chosen to be courageous... You just never realized it. You bravely chased after me when they caught me in that net, and once me and your entire family were gone from this Earth, you found the strength to go on and love a new family."

"Yes, but then I lost them too."

"Perhaps," says Donkor, "but you bravely endured the dungeon, the ship, and the plantation. And even once here, you courageously ministered to those around you. And you dealt with Emmanuel; most people were scared of him, but you weren't."

"He was just angry."

"And you understood that."

"But what good is that now? He's dead."

"So, what will you do now, Abena?" Donkor asks. "What will you do now?"

"...I will just stay here and settle for this life like Sarah. And, I'm too afraid to go alone, so I will allow my fear to control me just like Freddy. Besides, I no longer have the motivation to go, I don't want to do anything anymore... just like Lisa. Oh, but when I wake up tomorrow morning and see that Jason and that Master," she says as she stands to her feet. "I swear, I will give them hell for what they did to my brother. I hate them two... those no-good rats."

"So, is that it?" says Ozigbodi. "You'll settle for living in fear, laziness, and hate? No, Abena... No! You're better than that... You deserved more, much more."

"Listen to your mother's words, Abena; she is right. You *do* deserve better... despite everything that has happened, you still deserved better... but you have to see that for yourself."

"And we pray you will," Ozigbodi adds.

Donkor and Ozigbodi then vanish into thin air. Karina, now alone, looks to the ground and says aloud, "I've been through so much... so much." As she continues to stare, Ruth's words come to mind. Karina remembers hearing Ruth say, "Here in this lifetime, we experience what I call troubled waters... and there are various ways God will choose to help us with those troubled waters. Sometimes God will move troubled waters out of our way like he did for Moses and the children of Israel. Other times, he will cause us to rise above and walk on those troubled waters like he did for Peter when he was stuck in the middle of the deep. And then there are times when God will just make sure we have a paddle and a boat. He won't move problems out of our way, nor will he cause us to rise above them; he will just make sure we have the strength we need to endure them. So, with that being said..." She then imagines Ruth saying, "What will you do? What will you do Karina? What will you do?"

"What will you do, Abena?" she imagines hearing Donkor say.

"What will you do?" she then imagines hearing Ozigbodi say.

"What will you do? She then visualizes hearing Kevin say.

"Throughout the course of my lifetime," Karina then says while still staring at the ground, "I have found myself surrounded by many troubled waters... troubled waters that nearly forced me to surrender. Yet in the midst of my pain and sorrow; I am *making, a decision*...

"Tonight, I am deciding to not settle for less, but instead... aim for the best. And as I do, I will not allow fear, laziness, or even hate to stop me. Yes, in the course of my lifetime, *I have* experienced many troubled waters; troubled waters that almost had me surrender. However, I will not live in defeat," she says as she picks her head up and begins looking forward. "No... I won't! Because tonight... I am making, a decision. Tonight... I am choosing... to be... *courageous*. I *will* go to that house on top of the mountain. I should. I can. I will..."

For a moment, Karina looks straight ahead without saying a word. She then takes off running toward the entrance of the plantation. However, when she reaches Ehmerney's house, she is caught off guard by a barking dog. Looking at the dog, she sees that the animal is aggressively barking at her while chained to one of the porch's posts.

Chapter 3

"A dog!" she says as she looks wide-eyed. "When did Master get a dog?"

"Shhhh," she then sounds as she tries her best to silence it. "Hush," she says. "Hush!"

Suddenly, someone grabs Karina from behind. Startled, she begins to scream, but her cry is muffled when they place a hand over her mouth and then pull her behind a nearby tree.